ART and INVENTION

Inventions in Computing

From the Abacus to Personal Computers

Rachel Keranen

Cavendish Square
New York

Published in 2017 by Cavendish Square Publishing, LLC
243 5th Avenue, Suite 136, New York, NY 10016

First Edition

Website: cavendishsq.com

CPSIA Compliance Information: Batch #CW17CSQ

All websites were available and accurate when this book was sent to press.

Library of Congress Cataloging-in-Publication Data

Names: Keranen, Rachel, author.
Title: Inventions in computing : from the abacus to personal computers / Rachel Keranen.
Description: New York : Cavendish Square Publishing, [2017] | Series: Art and invention | Includes bibliographical references and index.
Identifiers: LCCN 2016026818 (print) | LCCN 2016030302 (ebook) |
ISBN 9781502623010 (library bound) | ISBN 9781502623027 (E-book)
Subjects: LCSH: Computer science--History--Juvenile literature.
Classification: LCC QA76.23 .K47 2017 (print) | LCC QA76.23 (ebook) | DDC 004--dc23
LC record available at https://lccn.loc.gov/2016026818

Editorial Director: David McNamara
Editor: Caitlyn Miller
Copy Editor: Nathan Heidelberger
Associate Art Director: Amy Greenan
Designer: Joseph Macri
Production Coordinator: Karol Szymczuk
Photo Research: J8 Media

The photographs in this book are used by permission and through the courtesy of: Cover Mark Wilson/Getty Images; p. 6-7 Computer Music Magazine/FutureGetty Images; p. 10 Sander de Wilde/Corbis News/Getty Images; p. 14 Sidhe/Shutterstock.com; p. 18 Eduard Kim/Shutterstock.com; p. 23 ThomasLENNE/Shutterstock.com; p. 24 ╨ö╨╗╨╕╤ÅΓÇ╨╡╨╝ ╨Ü╨╛╤ü╨╗╤Å╤å╨╛ ╨╛/iStock/Thinkstock; p. 27 Wilhelm Kubitschek/Wikimedia Commons/File:Salaminische Tafel Salamis Tablet nach Wilhelm Kubitschek Numismatische Zeitschrift Bd 31 Wien 1899 p. 394 ff.jpg; pp. 30,64 Science & Society Picture Library/Getty Images; p. 33 View Stock/Getty Images; p. 36 IrinaKorsakova/Shutterstock.com; p. 39 DEA PICTURE LIBRARY/De Agostini/Getty Images; p. 445-45 hujiie/Shutterstock.com; p. 49 claudiodivizia/iStock/Thinkstock; p. 50 Everett Collection; p. 56-57 TedColes/Wikimedia Commons/File:Frontal view of the reconstructed Colossus at The National Museum of Computing, Bletchley Park.jpg; p. 67 Justin Sullivan/Getty Images; p. 68 Future Publishing/Getty Images; p. 72 SGM/Shutterstyock.com; p. 78 betto Rodrigues/Shutterstock.com; p. 83 Pacific Press/LightRocket/Getty Images; p. 85 Chris Farina/Corbis News/Getty Images; p. 89 Tighef/Wikimedia Commons/File:View inside detector at the CMS cavern LHC CERN.jpg; p. 92-93 SKatzenberger/Shutterstock.com.

Printed in the United States of America

CONTENTS

INTRODUCTION: Art and Innovations

"A man in his house does not live on the staircase, but makes use of it to go up and down and gain access to every room. The human mind, likewise, does not reside in numbers, but uses them to attain all sciences and arts."

—Antoine de Rivarol

In the world of personal computing, one name towers above the rest: Apple. Our iPhones and MacBooks help us send text messages, share carefully edited Instagram posts, and create beautiful computer graphics and animations. The iPhones and MacBooks themselves have a recognizable aesthetic: they are sleek, elegant, and minimalist.

It's no mistake that the Apple products many of us use daily are both well designed and well suited for design. Apple's cofounder Steve Jobs lived to find the intersection of art and computing. While his cofounder Steve Wozniak focused on making computers that worked better than any others at the time, it was Jobs who obsessed over the rounded edges of the first Apples and the material of the cases. It was Jobs who encouraged his design team to think of themselves as artists who created for a mass audience, just as Tiffany mass-produced beautiful glass lamps. Since the beginnings of our species, dreamers like Jobs have propelled technology forward as a means to make better or different art.

Before there could be any personal computing technology, there first had to be numbers. It's easy to take numbers, counting, and simple math for granted, but there was a time when humans didn't have number systems. When number systems did emerge, the earliest numbers looked very different than the numbers we know today. Early numbers appeared in the form of symbols that represented daily objects; the Romans later turned to letters to represent amounts. It wasn't until about the twelfth century that the digits 0 through 9, invented in India, arrived in Europe from the Middle East. A few centuries later, the mathematician and philosopher Gottfried Wilhelm Leibniz popularized the **binary** number system, which would become the foundation for all modern computers.

In the midst of the Industrial Revolution, automation, mass production, and speed became essential to maintaining a competitive edge. The silk weavers of Lyon, France, wanted to automate their work, which was slow and required at least two people per loom. In the early nineteenth century, the silk weaver Joseph-Marie Jacquard invented a loom that could process instructions to create intricately woven tapestries at a groundbreaking speed. Jacquard used **punch cards**, which could represent the commands "lift threads" or "don't lift threads" to communicate the design to the automated loom. In doing so, Jacquard became the first to successfully refine and sell an automated loom design that had been in the works for the past half a century.

Punch cards became the basis for early computers and were used in computers until the middle of the twentieth century. When Kenneth Knowlton invented the first computer animation language in the 1960s, it was on a computer that relied on punch cards. Knowlton's first language, while the first step in computer animation,

A 2013 Pew Research survey found that 84 percent of American households own a computer.

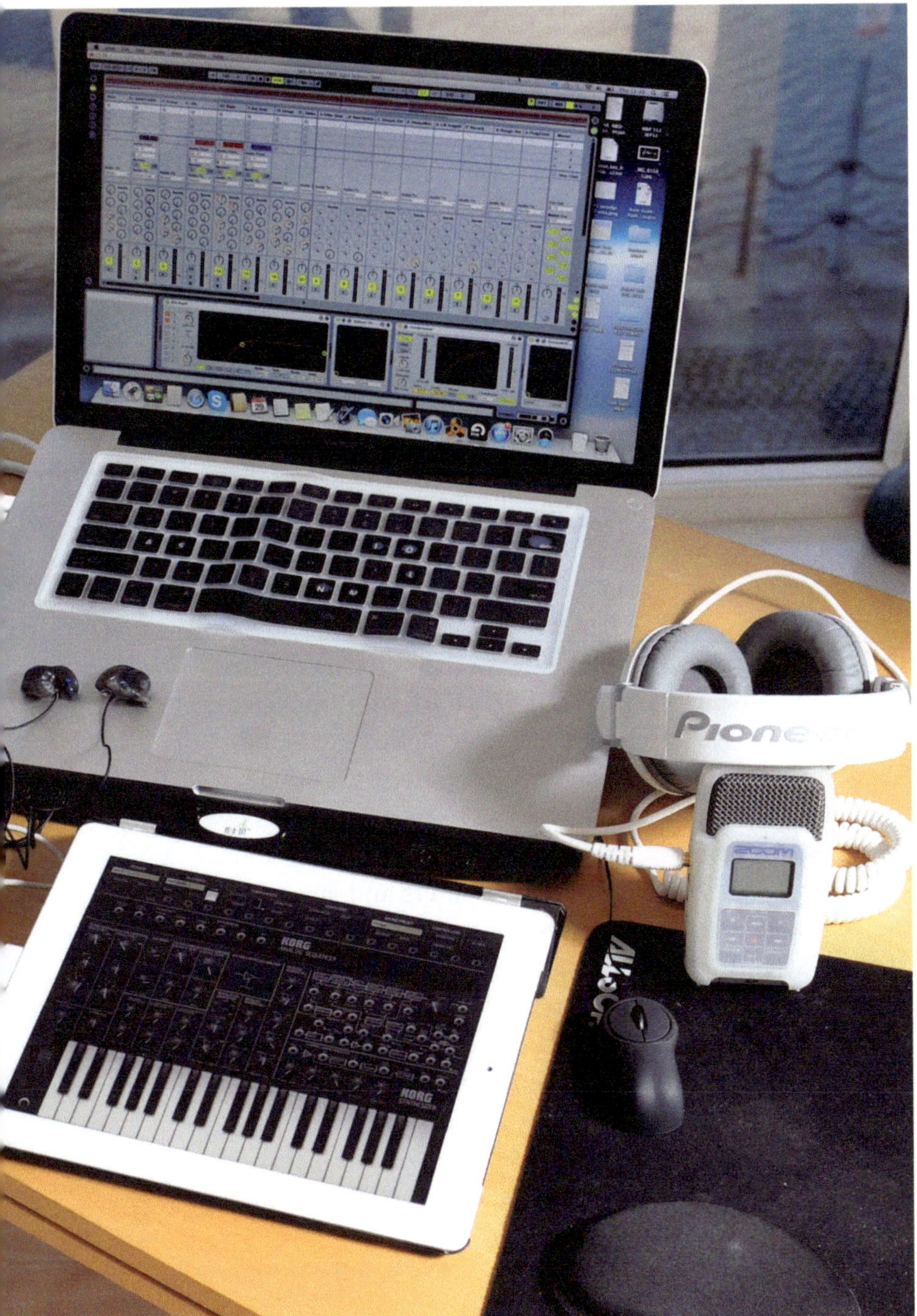

had limited applications. He worked with artist Lillian Schwartz to make a second computer animation programming language, which she used to produce award-winning animations. After Knowlton and Schwartz's animated computer films, the computer animation industry took off over the next few decades to bring us the animated films we know so well today, from the early pioneers *Beauty and the Beast* and *Toy Story* to *Shrek* and *How to Train Your Dragon*.

Computer animation was aided by progress in personal computers, a revolution launched by Steve Jobs (who also spent time as CEO of pioneering computer animation film studio Pixar), his cofounder Steve Wozniak, and their company Apple Computer. For decades, computers were extremely expensive and remained in the realm of businesses and universities. They were also huge and inaccessible to the average consumer. They had no attached monitor, and users had no intuitive way to interact with them. Jobs, Wozniak, and Apple ushered in the era of **graphical user interfaces** (screens with visual elements like icons and images) and affordable, user-friendly personal computers.

Personal computing had a huge impact on the art world, opening up the desktop publishing industry and allowing artists to use desktop computers and laptops to create graphic designs, edit photos and films, and more. It also paved the way for smaller computers in the form of smartphones, music players, and tablets, which again created new ways to make and share art. The first iPhones (and other smartphones) had limited resolution and data storage, but through subsequent releases, the cameras and tools within the phones have improved such that photographer Annie Leibovitz called the iPhone 4 the best point-and-shoot camera of its time.

As we look forward to the future of art and computers, we can anticipate advances in the developing industries of

virtual reality (VR) and 3D printing. Both technologies already exist and are in the process of becoming cheaper, more versatile, and more accessible to artists and a wider consumer audience. Some artists are using VR to create new environments in the virtual world in which they can create and share art, while some companies, including Google, have released tools that allow any artist to step into a virtual environment and create new forms of art. Meanwhile, 3D printing allows artists, especially jewelry and fashion designers, to create using new materials and means of production.

Other interesting projects in art and computing include computer-created art, in which programmers create software programs and algorithms that then allow computers to create paintings and musical compositions, both in the style of famous artists and in their own style.

Educational institutions from CalArts, the school founded by Walt Disney, to Stanford have introduced majors that combine art and computing. After centuries of computing developments led or affected by artists, these institutions have recognized the importance of teaching artists technical skills. They have also recognized the importance of teaching programmers the creative skills that can shape the products they build going forward.

Beyond art, computers now affect nearly every aspect of our lives. As computers become increasingly powerful and sophisticated and progressively smaller and cheaper to produce, advances in computing will shape how we work, travel, spend money, receive health care, and so much more.

The real Ishango Bone is kept at the Museum of Natural Sciences in Brussels, Belgium. Shown here is a 23-foot (7-meter) replica in Brussels.

CHAPTER 1
A History of Numbers

In the era before the first **abacus**, computing was extremely limited compared to today's standards. Yet early civilizations did not have much need for advanced computing. At first, there were no numbers or mathematics. As people moved into cities and began trading, storing, and dividing wealth, numbers and calculations appeared in the record of human history. Calculations then became more important in tracking the complex relationships between individuals, businesses, and institutions, as well as for studying mathematics, physics, and other sciences.

Today, we encounter two primary number systems in our daily lives, though most of us are only aware of our interactions with one of those systems: the **Hindu-Arabic numeral** system. The system is composed of ten digits from 0 to 9. Every time we use a computer or smartphone, however, the electronic device operates using a binary number system with two digits, 0 and 1. Most of us are also familiar with the Roman numeral system, though we use it infrequently. The earliest numbers appeared far before even the Roman numeral system emerged.

The FIRST NUMBERS

We'll never know exactly who the first person to count was or what objects they counted, but scholars believe it's likely they used their fingers to keep track of how many objects they were representing. The first archaeological evidence of a mathematical aid dates back to about twenty thousand years ago.

In 1950, a Belgian geologist named Jean de Heinzelin de Braucourt discovered a fibula bone topped with a fragment of quartz. It is called the Ishango Bone, and it was found in what was then the Belgian colony of the Congo (now the Democratic Republic of Congo). The bone is about 4 inches (10 centimeters) long with carved notches, indicating its use as what's called a **tally stick**.

Scientists believe that the Ishango Bone is the oldest known mathematical object and that the notches indicate more than just basic accounting. The notches on one side are organized in groups of three and six ($3 \times 2 = 6$), four and eight ($4 \times 2 = 8$), and five and ten ($5 \times 2 = 10$). Scholars don't think this grouping is accidental—the bone suggests that its users knew how to multiply by two. The three individual sides of the bone contain sixty, forty-eight, and sixty notches each, all multiples of twelve. This, too, would be an unlikely coincidence and indicates some concept of mathematical patterns.

As humans moved from caves to constructed houses and the population in early civilizations grew, so too did the use of numbers and mathematics. Instead of notches, from around the eighth millennium BCE, ancient Middle Eastern societies began to use pebbles and later beads to represent counts. For each sheep that left a pen, for example, a pebble could be added to a heap. When it was time for the sheep to return, each pebble in that heap was moved until none remained. There may or may not have been any numbers or thoughts of numbers associated with this count. It was simply a way of representing how many sheep had been let out to pasture and needed to be brought back in at the end of the day. By using pebbles, people could subtract much more easily than was possible using other systems, like notched bones.

Eventually, the use of pebbles gave way to the use of shaped beads. These beads could be made into different shapes representing different values. This was a significant advance from the system of one stone = 1. It's an improvement that is easy to understand if you imagine carrying seventy-five individual pebbles representing seventy-five sheep versus a handful of beads representing seven groups of ten sheep and five single sheep.

In the ancient Sumerian and Elamite civilizations, the concepts of debts, payments, and properties began to require record keeping. The civilizations were ancient, but the societies had complex social structures and relationships. There were centrally stored grains that needed to be organized and distributed, profits and losses, and taxes that all required accurate records and arithmetic. From around the fourth millenium BCE, the common accounting method was to record amounts by placing beads in a clay pouch (called a **bulla**) and sealing it. However, after sealing the pouch, the number could not be read without breaking the pouch open.

Starting in about 3300 BCE, the practice included marking the amount inside the clay pouch with symbols on the outside of the clay pouch. Thus, the first accounting documents were born. The use of beads within the pouch quickly disappeared, as they were no longer necessary if the amounts were marked on the outside. Also, the first clay tablets emerged. Written symbols had replaced physical symbols.

The symbols varied by cultures. For example, the Elamites had used a stick to represent 1, a bead to represent 10, a disc to represent 100, a small cone to represent 300, and a large perforated cone to represent 3,000. The Sumerians, meanwhile, had used a small cone to represent 1, a bead to represent 10, a large cone to represent 60, a large perforated cone to represent 600,

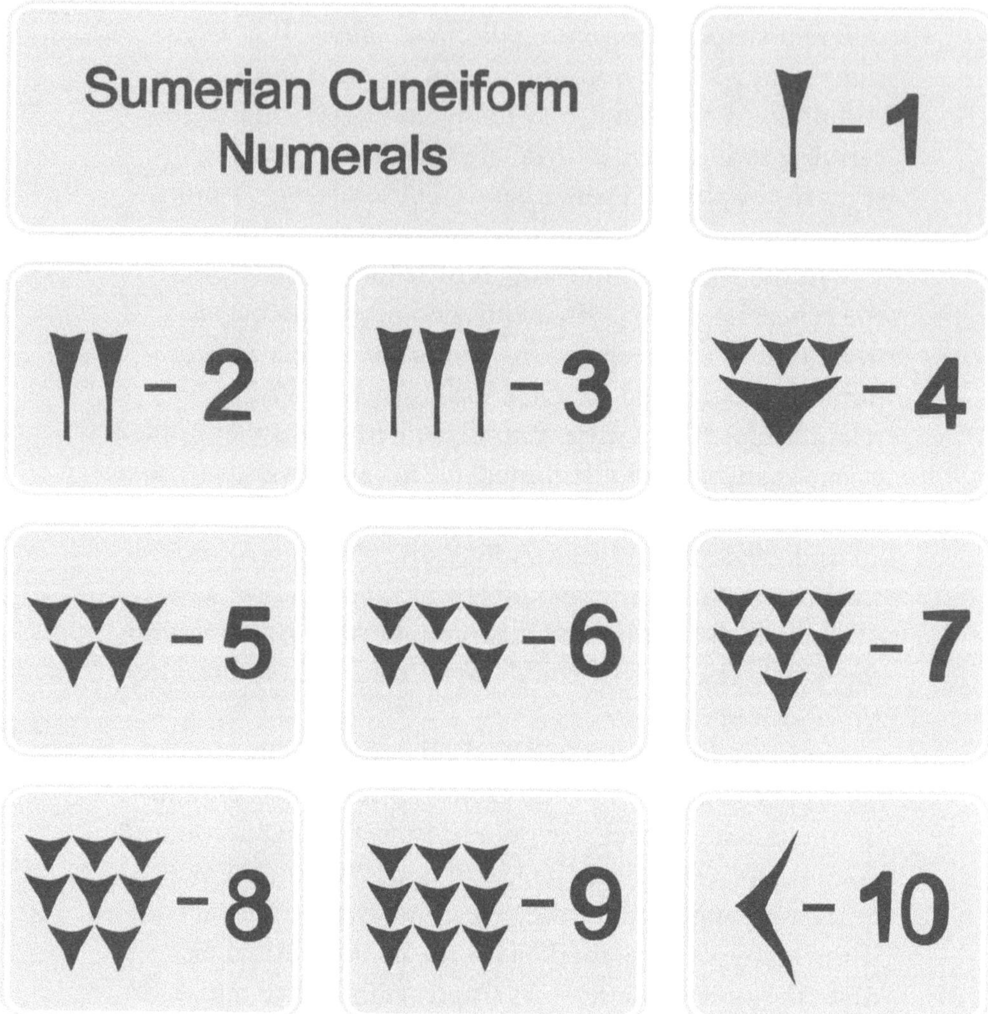

In addition to the cuneiform numbers shown here, the ancient Sumerians also had symbols for common fractions, including ½.

a sphere to represent 3,000, and a perforated sphere to represent 36,000. (As you can see, the Sumerian numbering system emphasized multiples of 60, creating what is known as a base-60 number system.) The first written number systems were symbols that mirrored these physical objects. In the third millenium BCE, these systems evolved into wedge-shaped signs.

Using these symbols, first physically represented and then recorded on tablets, those who knew math could add, subtract, multiply, and divide. Adding is straightforward: one Sumerian cone plus one bead is now one cone and one bead. Subtraction worked in the opposite way. Multiplication in its simplest form could be done by creating repeated groupings of symbols (such as four perforated cones and one bead) and then combining them. For larger numbers or faster calculations, it was useful to take advantage of the known relationships between the symbols. One Sumerian cone multiplied by ten, for example, was equivalent to one bead. One bead multiplied by six was equivalent to a large cone. Even if an amount wasn't being precisely multiplied by, say, ten, a large calculation could be broken into smaller calculations that took advantage of these relationships. Division was limited to simple, fraction-based division.

During this time, only a select group of society was educated in numbers, and they became the powerful elite.

Ancient Greek Mathematics

More complex mathematics came millennia later from ancient Greeks, including the mathematician and philosopher Pythagoras in the sixth century BCE.

Pythagoras moved from Greece to Italy in about 532 BCE and established a school in Croton (today Crotone). Pythagoras established the significance of numbers in the objective world and in music, such as the harmonious sound of some notes when played together in contrast to the disharmonious sounds of other pairings. The most harmonious pairings, he discovered, could be expressed in ratios of whole numbers, such as fourths, fifths, and octaves. Pythagoras is also often credited with inventing the Pythagorean theorem, which expresses the relationship between the three sides of a right triangle: $a^2 + b^2 = c^2$.

Roman Numerals

The ancient Greeks also had their own number system, which varied in form by island. Greece fell to the Romans in 146 BCE, and Roman culture was highly influenced by the Greek ways. They did not, however, adopt the Greek number system.

The ancient Romans used a number system that we still know today due to the spread and legacy of their empire: the Roman numerals I (1), V (5), X (10), and so on. The form "one less than," as represented by IV (4, or one less than 5), avoided the repetition of four characters in a row and made it easier to visually scan a number and understand its value.

Yet Roman numerals made it hard to represent very large numbers (try writing 1.34 billion in Roman numerals!) and cumbersome to perform calculations.

Hindu-Arabic Numerals

Meanwhile, a new numeral system was in use in India that was much better suited to representing large numbers and performing arithmetic. Its superiority, in fact, makes it very familiar to us today. It contained ten digits, ranging from 0 to 9. Now, instead of two beads or two notches, two individual units could be summarized as one digit, 2. With just ten symbols, the Indians were able to represent the very smallest and very largest numbers imaginable. And for the first time, there was a refined concept of the number 0, which had no value but affected the values of numbers that contained it. (The ancient Babylonians also added a sign for zero sometime between the fourth and first centuries BCE, but it was only used between two other numbers, such as 306, and never at the end, such as 330.)

Indians had been using their system since at least 500 BCE. The advantages of the system helped Indian scientists beat Western scientists to many theories, including the theory that Earth spins on an axis and that Earth moves around the sun. They also calculated the diameter of the globe within 1 percent of its actual diameter.

The Indian system made its way west and arrived in Baghdad in about 762 CE. The Muslim religion was about one hundred years old at the time (it began in 610 CE), and early Islamic scholars brought books on astronomy and mathematics from India to Baghdad, a cultural center of the Islamic world. Over the next few centuries, the Islamic empire grew culturally and scientifically.

In the ninth century CE, a Persian mathematician and astronomer Muhammad ibn Musa al-Khwarizmi wrote several influential books on mathematics. Al-Khwarizmi lived in Baghdad and worked at the House of Wisdom, which published original research and translated scientific and philosophical works. Many of al-Khwarizmi's books, including *Al-kitab al-mukhtaṣar fi ḥisab al-jabr wal-muqabala* (*The Compendious Book on Calculation by Completion and Balancing*), were translated from Arabic to Latin in the twelfth century. The *Compendious* included instruction on algebra and geometry, including how to use algebra to determine inheritances based on Islamic law. (The word "algorithm" comes from his name in Latin.)

In another book, translated into Latin in the twelfth century as *Algoritmi de numero Indorum* (*Al-Khwarizmi*

Muhammad ibn Musa al-Khwarizmi, honored by this monument in Uzbekistan, was one of many influential scholars in the Islamic Golden Age.

Concerning the Hindu Art of Reckoning), the mathematician described Indian numerals and arithmetic. Al-Khwarizmi's work helped European mathematicians and scientists succeed in mathematics after Europe emerged from the Dark Ages.

The Indian system has been referred to as the Arabic numeral system, which reflects its arrival in Europe via the Arabic world. Today, the system is usually referred to by scholars as the Hindu-Arabic numeral system.

The Spread of Hindu-Arabic Numerals in the West

The very first instances of the Hindu-Arabic numerals in Europe date back to texts in Spain after the Moorish invasion that occurred in 711 CE. It wasn't until the twelfth century onward, however, that the Hindu-Arabic numerals began to spread more significantly in Europe. The spread of the system was through translated works by al-Khwarizmi and other scholars. These important intellectuals included Leonardo Pisano, better known as Fibonacci. At the time, while al-Khwarizmi's works had been translated into Latin, only a handful of European intellectuals knew the Hindu-Arabic numeral system.

Fibonacci (which means "Son of Bonacci"), was a medieval mathematician born in Pisa, Italy, but educated in Algeria in northern Africa, where his father was a diplomat and public notary. He also traveled through Egypt, Syria, Greece, Sicily, and Provence, where he learned different number systems and mathematics.

"There, when I had been introduced to the art of the Indians' nine symbols through remarkable teaching, knowledge of the art very soon pleased me above all else and I came to understand it," Fibonacci wrote in *Liber abaci* (*Book of Calculations*), published in 1202. The book

The FIRST WRITTEN WORDS

The first writing system appeared around 3500 BCE in Mesopotamia, home to the earliest known civilizations founded on the land between the Tigris and Euphrates Rivers in modern day Iraq, Syria, and Kuwait.

The first words, like the first numbers, were used for commercial and administrative purposes and consisted of pictures of real-life objects, or **pictographs.** Many of the earliest pictographs are undecipherable, but some clearly illustrate rations to be counted, such as a grain of barley or a fish. The system required people to memorize hundreds or thousands of pictographs to communicate and consisted largely of nouns.

Pictographs evolved into cuneiform writing, which involved using a reed stylus to impress wedge-shaped signs into clay tablets. It's harder to make curved lines than straight lines in clay, so the symbols were very linear. Writing became increasingly phonetic (written words reflected spoken pronunciation instead of symbolizing objects), which allowed writers to communicate more abstract concepts including names and ideas. Cuneiform writing allowed writers to tell stories and record histories. In fact, the *Epic of Gilgamesh*, which tells the story of a Sumerian king, was written in cuneiform.

The written word evolved out of the practice of numbers-based accounting, but curiously, once abacus-based mathematics became the norm in Europe, those who didn't know how to read and write were more suspicious of math done on "pen and paper." (Understandably so—if you don't understand how someone is arriving at the amount you owe them, it's an uncomfortable situation.) They preferred to see the visual representations of amounts and calculations performed on stones and tablets.

discusses the use and advantages of the Hindu-Arabic numbers and the arithmetic and algebra Fibonacci had learned in northern Africa. (Fibonacci is also famous for introducing the Fibonacci sequence, a series of numbers where each number is the sum of the two preceding numbers: 0, 1, 1, 2, 3, 5, 8, and so on. The Fibonacci sequence is often represented in nature by arrangements such as the branching of trees, and it is also used today in computer algorithms.)

Fibonacci wrote several other books, including *Practica geometriae* and *Liber quadratorum*, which were significant in boosting the European mathematics scene. His works were read widely in Europe, where capitalism and the accompanying trade and accounting were beginning to thrive.

Even as knowledge of the Hindu-Arabic numeral system spread among the more educated Europeans, the system and its methods of calculation did not become popular until the seventeenth or eighteenth centuries. This timing is partly due to the lack of widespread popular education until after the sixteenth century. Many in medieval Europe could not read or write, and therefore "reckoning" with counters (using stones or disks and counting boards, which are covered in more detail in the next chapter) was more accessible than calculating through pen-and-paper (or pen-and-**parchment**) means. When people who didn't understand the Hindu-Arabic numerals completed financial transactions with those who did, they were hesitant to use a new number system that they could not understand. The city of Florence went so far as to ban the use of Hindu-Arabic numerals in 1299.

The slow adoption also reflects the difficulty many people had in understanding the concept of zero, a number that had no value but added value when inserted between or after numbers. One of the Latin words for zero was *ciphra* (from the Arabic *as-sifr* or *sifr*).

Eventually, due to the term's mysteriousness, this became the English word for a secret code—a cipher. Other factors include general resistance to change and the Arabic, non-Christian roots of the system as viewed by a deeply religious, Christian Europe.

For a time, both Arabic arithmetic and the counters method were included in textbooks. Slowly, however, the ease of writing and calculating with Hindu-Arabic numerals eventually replaced Roman numerals. By the sixteenth century, Hindu-Arabic numerals were commonly used in commerce and taught in schools. By the seventeenth century, most western European record keepers had transitioned to Hindu-Arabic numerals.

The Binary Number System

In 1679, the German mathematician Gottfried Wilhelm Leibniz invented (or at least refined) the modern binary system. Leibniz had already done significant work in the field of calculus and built a multiplication machine that he presented to the Royal Society in London. He was inspired to create the binary number system by the Chinese *I Ching* and its concepts of yin and yang.

The binary number system is a base-two system with two digits: 0 and 1. For those who aren't familiar with binary, the numbers can be perplexing. The decimal number 12, for example, is equivalent to 1100 in binary. Electronic machines understand binary code very well, as the system can represent the presence (1) or absence (0) of an electrical charge.

Numbers and Computing

As we will see in the next two chapters, the numbers and number systems we have directly impact the type

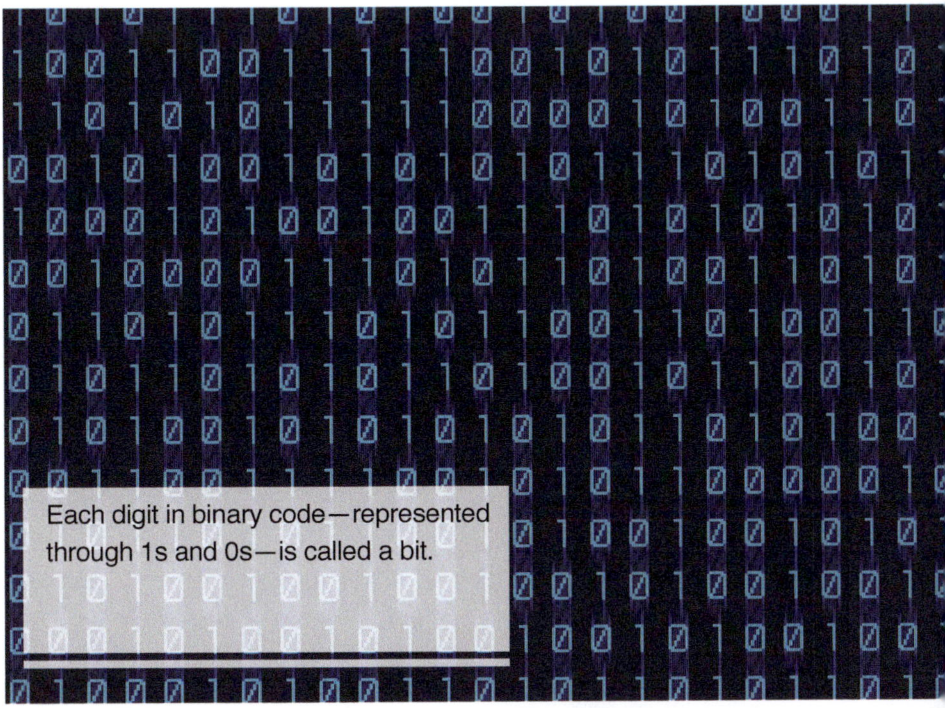

Each digit in binary code—represented through 1s and 0s—is called a bit.

of calculations and computing we can do. Sumerian, Greek, and Roman numerals all lent themselves better to abacus methods (both the board abacus and bead abacus). However, the popularization of the Hindu-Arabic numeral system pretty much ended the use of the abacus in the West. Meanwhile, the invention of binary opened new doors to communicating with machines. It became the basis for modern computers.

The bead abacus can be used to find square roots and cubic roots in addition to basic arithmetic.

CHAPTER 2
The Abacus

Today when we think of tablets, we often think of devices like the iPad or various Android models. The first tablet in the history of computing, the abacus, had a significantly different form and function.

There are two major styles of abacus: the table abacus (also called a counting board) with counters, and the bead abacus. Many people are more familiar with the bead abacus, which was first found in Rome almost two millennia ago and is still used in Asian countries today. The table abacus is its precursor and dates back much farther.

The BIRTHPLACE of the ABACUS

It's thought that the earliest version of the abacus was a board or slab spread with sand that Sumerians used to write on sometime between 2700 BCE and 2300 BCE. Indeed, the word "abacus" comes from the Semitic word *abaq* or *abk*, meaning "sand" or "dust." This morphed into the Greek word *abax*, meaning "table" or "tablet," before reaching its current form. This first ancient abacus was suited primarily for addition and subtraction.

At the time, Sumer was one of two civilizations in the ancient region of Babylonia. The Sumerians lived in cities with residential districts, plant and animal agriculture, and specialized industries including carpentry, shipbuilding, pottery, and textiles. They traded with other civilizations, and some Sumerians received rations from a central supply of resources in return for their daily work.

Sumerian city-states were often at war with each other and with the other Babylonian civilization, Akkad. Despite the fighting, the Sumerians made significant cultural contributions to humanity. They invented the first system of writing (described in the previous chapter), along with literary, musical, and architectural forms that would influence Western civilization going forward, and much more—including the first abacus.

Over time, the abacus evolved to become better suited for counting, and its use spread throughout the ancient world. Though no archaeological evidence of abacus boards has been found in Egypt, the ancient Greek historian Herodotus describes Egyptian use of the abacus. The oldest discovered abacus comes from the island of Salamis in Greece.

The Ancient Abacus

In ancient times, performing calculations looked very different than the process does today. Today, we learn how to calculate the price of 4 pounds (1.8 kilograms) of apples that cost two dollars per pound by writing down the equation in Hindu-Arabic numerals and performing the arithmetic: $4 \times 2 = 8$. (Of course, such a simple equation is possible using mental math, but we learn to calculate with much larger numbers in the same way, carrying numbers as we work out the solution.) With a computer, such calculations are even easier to perform.

It's only been during the last several hundred years, however, that the common approach was to write down a

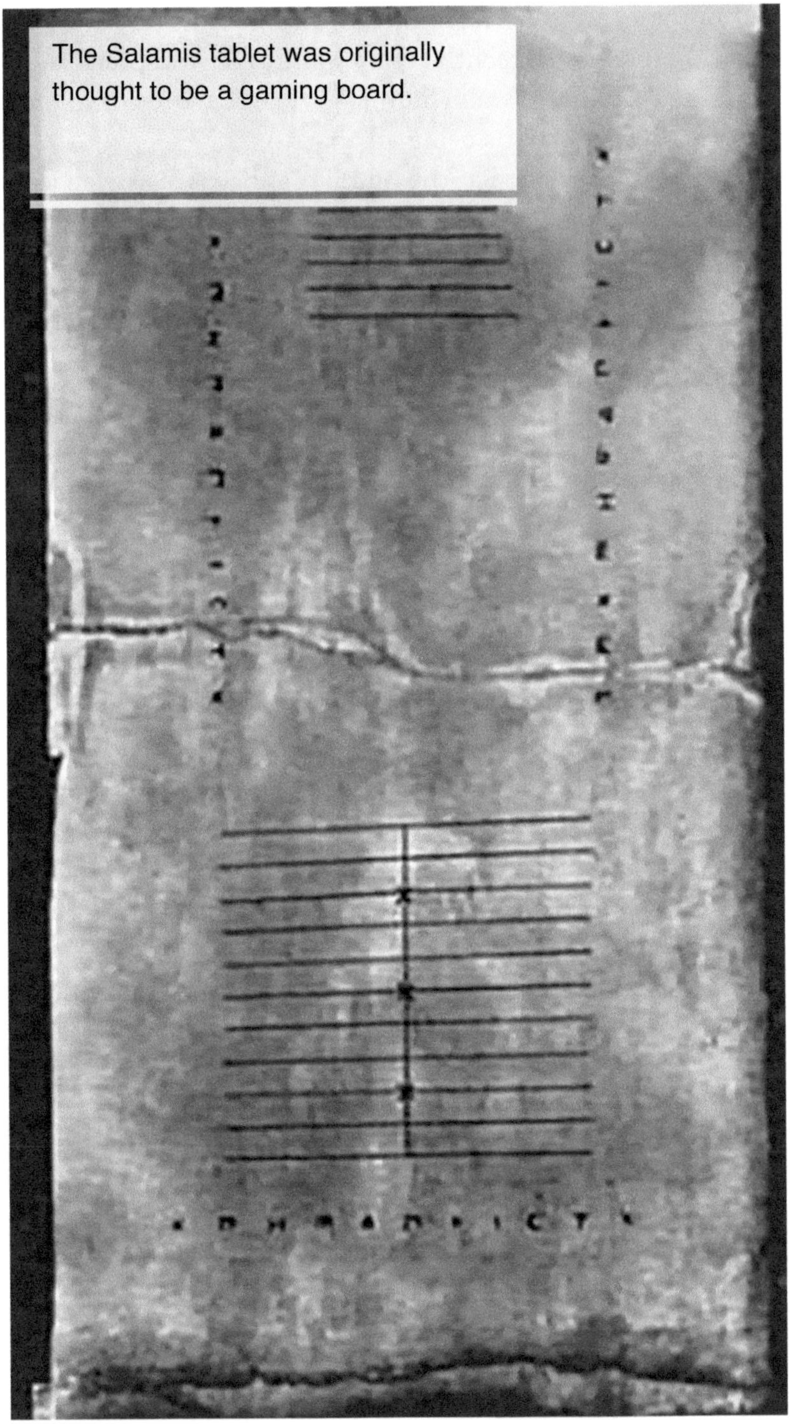

The Salamis tablet was originally thought to be a gaming board.

math problem and perform the arithmetic with pen and paper. Before the sixteenth century and the widespread adoption of Hindu-Arabic numerals, it was more common to perform calculations using an abacus.

Ancient Greek abaci (the plural of "abacus"), as well as ancient Roman abaci, were typically tables or boards made of marble or wood with carved or painted lines that marked place values (1s, 10s, 100s, and so on). Paired with pebbles or other counting pieces, the abacus was a common tool for merchants in outdoor markets.

The earliest archaeological evidence of the abacus is the Greek abaci that date back to the fifth century BCE. The most famous of these Greek abaci is the Salamis tablet, named for the island on which it was found. The Salamis tablet is a white marble slab nearly 5 feet (1.5 meters) long and about 2.5 feet (0.75 m) wide, ranging from about 2 to 4 inches (5 to 10 cm) thick. It has Greek numerical symbols on three sides, scaling from 1 to 1,000 on one side and from 1/8 of an obol to 6,000 drachmae on the other two sides. (Obols and drachmae were units of both weight and money in ancient Greece.) It has two sets of parallel horizontal lines, each divided by a vertical line. The lines are spaced such that it would be very easy to put pebbles on and between lines to represent value.

The abacus was not a calculator or computer in itself, but a tool to aid humans in their calculations before written arithmetic using Hindu-Arabic numbers was possible. By placing counters such as pebbles in the columns of the abacus, merchants could move the counters around the board or table while making large calculations, such as tracking preliminary sums, carrying numbers, and calculating remainders. The abacus could help with anything from simple arithmetic to more complicated calculations, such as the interest due on a principal sum over a period of time.

In some cases, to make it easier to visually scan the value represented on an abacus, a single counter might be placed slightly offset from a column to represent 5 (or 50 or 500). The layout technique is much like the intermediate symbols V, L, and D in the Roman numeral system that represent 5, 50, and 500. In fact, in Roman abaci, the layout of counters on the abacus corresponded quite well with the Roman numeral system—a board with two counters in the "ones" column, three counters in the "tens" column, and one counter in the "hundreds" column would represent the same value as CXXXII, or 132. Visually, the counters more closely approximate their Roman numeral equivalent than their Hindu-Arabic equivalent.

There are no clear remnants of Roman counting board abaci (boards made of wood could have easily been destroyed, and stone tablets could have worn down or faded), but there are examples of Roman **calculi**, the counters used in calculations. (The Latin word *calx* means "pebble" or "stone," a meaning we can see today in the word "calcium." The original tradition of using pebbles as counters shows how the mathematical word "calculus" has the same root as the mineral word "calcium.") These Roman calculi were flat or slightly rounded disks that could easily slide over the boards, about 0.5 to 0.75 inches (13 to 19 millimeters) in diameter and made from materials such as bone, ivory, or glass.

The Ancient Roman Pocket Calculator

A few examples exist of a Roman abacus from the first century CE that was small enough to fit in the palm of one's hand. Its construction varied significantly from the traditional table- or tablet-style abaci of the time. The Roman pocket abacus was made of a small metal plate with beads that moved in parallel slots from side to side. Each slot represented place values.

The portable Roman abacus was especially useful for bankers, businesspeople, and engineers.

The pocket abacus looks more like the Eastern bead abaci that appeared centuries later and are still in use today. It's possible that the bead-based abacus spread from the Romans to the Chinese through their trade relationships along the Silk Road. However, there is no definitive connection between the Roman and Chinese abaci, and it's possible that the two abaci developed independently.

Later Use of the Abacus in Western Europe

The abacus spread from Rome to England and, in the thirteenth century CE, from England to France, where it was used until the transition from Roman numerals to Hindu-Arabic numerals fully took place. (The struggle

CLASSICAL GREECE

The Salamis tablet and the other earliest known abaci date back to the Classical Age in Greece, which began in 510 BCE. Shortly before the Classical Age began, the city-state of Athens saw a number of changes.

In the beginning of the sixth century BCE, the Athenians lost an attempt to control the island of Salamis. Salamis was situated between Athens and the rival Greek city-state of Megara. An Athenian poet and merchant named Solon encouraged the Athenians by reciting a poem he had written. He wanted the city-state to rally from a loss they had suffered against the Megarians. Led by Solon, the Athenians resumed the war. They eventually won control of Salamis. Around 594 BCE, having won the loyalty of Athenians for unifying them toward victory, Solon became archon (annual chief ruler). He began implementing many reforms.

At the time, Athens faced many economic and political problems. The wealthy controlled the government, excluding the middle class and forcing the poorest into serfdom or slavery. According to the law, people who couldn't pay their debts could be enslaved. Almost all crimes were punishable by death. Many in debt fled Athens, and the city-state faced an uncertain future.

As archon, Solon freed enslaved debtors and passed measures designed to promote trade and industry. He implemented a new system of weights and measures and encouraged foreign tradesmen to settle in Athens. He counted the population by dividing citizens into four groups. These groups were based on annual income (which included amounts of grain, oil, wine, and money). He banned the export of agricultural products other than olive oil to reduce food shortages. And he also helped create Athens's reputation as a producer and exporter of olive oil, wine, and fine pottery. It is easy to see how important counting, calculations, and numbers must have been for Athenians in this period of great change!

between those who used the abacus to perform arithmetic and those who used new methods was fierce and included open competitions between the techniques.)

Counter boards and tables remain from this time, as do metal counters used for reckoning. These special metal counters were called jettons in England and *jetons* in France. The name comes from the French word *jeter*, which means "to throw" or "to cast."

The jettons often had emblems or fleur-de-lis motifs on them. Some expressed loyalty to a house; others showed the heads of English or French monarchs. At first, the English jettons were made in France. From the sixteenth century onward, however, most English jettons were produced in Nuremburg, Germany, and the designs were often inaccurate. In eighteenth-century France, however, jetons took on more artistic value. Some jetons were made in bronze, silver, or even gold. Important French families might have a custom-designed set made for their house.

The EASTERN ABACUS

The earliest reference to an abacus in the East comes from documents dating back to the second century BCE that mention an abacus made from bamboo sticks placed on squares of a checkerboard and the process of "calculating with rods."

Documents from the thirteenth century CE, many centuries later, are the first to illustrate the use of the Chinese bead abacus, called the *suan pan*. The suan pan has a rectangular frame made of wood with thirteen vertical rods and wooden balls divided by a horizontal beam. Each rod represents a power of ten increasing in power as you move to the left. There are two beads above the beam on each rod and five beads below. The top beads each represent five units, the bottom beads each represent one unit. (For

The top beads in the *suan pan* are sometimes called heaven beads, while the bottom beads are called earth beads.

example, the number six can be represented using one top bead and one bottom bead.)

To use the suan pan, you first place the suan pan on a flat surface and move all the beads above the beam to the top of the frame and all of the beads below the beam to the bottom of the frame. Then, to represent the number 2, for example, you move two bottom beads on the rightmost rod toward the center horizontal rod. To add 2 + 1, you then move one bead on the rightmost rod up. Now, there are three beads toward the center of the rightmost rod. This is a very simple calculation for the sake of illustration, but those who use the suan pan regularly become very fast at representing enormous numbers and moving beads to do addition, subtraction, multiplication, and division.

Over the next few centuries, the suan pan migrated from China to Korea (where it is called the *jupan* or *supan*) and then to Japan. The Japanese *soroban* is similar to the Chinese suan pan, except the soroban has just one bead above the horizontal beam and four below. (A top bead was removed first, followed by the removal of a bottom bead in the 1930s.)

The remaining beads still allow any number to be represented, as the number 9 can be represented using the single top bead, which represents five units, and the four bottom beads, which represent one unit each. (The extra beads in the Chinese abacus allow operators to quickly represent intermediate results above nine, however, and the change in design requires a different abacus technique.) The soroban also has a dot on every third rod to indicates units, such as the decimal place or place value (as a comma does in the number 3,123).

The Japanese soroban was first used by merchants and wasn't popularly used until the seventeenth century. Today, Japan has tens of thousands of abacus clubs and an All-Japan National Soroban Championship. While students could, of course, use computers or more advanced calculators to perform their calculations, using an abacus has many benefits. Using an abacus requires memorization and concentration. (Japanese students regularly rank among the highest in the world on standardized math tests, along with South Korea and other Asian nations.) Some of the elderly in Japan also use the soroban as a way to stay sharp.

Other countries that use similar bead abaci include Russia, Iran, Turkey, Afghanistan, and Armenia.

From ABACI to COMPUTERS

The abacus is not a computer as it's entirely dependent on the thought processes of the human using it. It is, however, important as an early aid to counting and calculations. Later, mathematicians and scholars would try repeatedly to invent calculating machines that would make complex calculations easier to solve. Wilhelm Schickard invented a calculating clock in 1623, which was lost to a fire. Blaise Pascal invented the Arithmetic Machine in the 1640s, which could perform addition and subtraction. Leibniz invented the Step Reckoner in 1673, which could perform multiplication. The Industrial Revolution in the eighteenth century sparked even greater desire for such calculating machines. As a result, a very different type of machine emerged: an automated loom that would shape the future of modern computers.

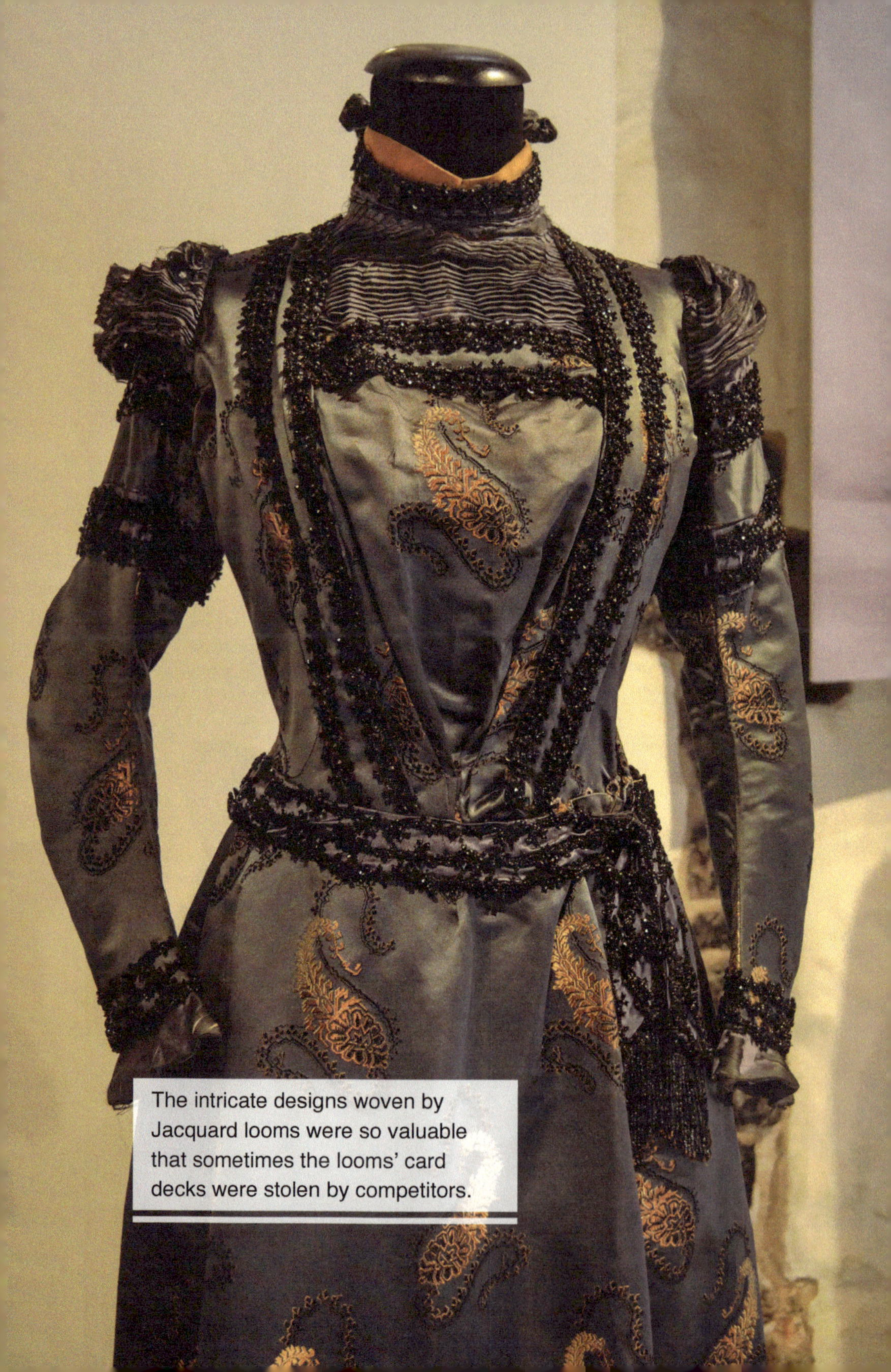

The intricate designs woven by Jacquard looms were so valuable that sometimes the looms' card decks were stolen by competitors.

CHAPTER 3
The Jacquard Loom

The Industrial Revolution, which began around 1760 in Britain, was a time of great change in manufacturing. There were new materials, power sources, and technologies that made it significantly easier to mass-produce goods. Britain was the first to industrialize and was the only country that had many of the new technologies. Yet soon enough, industrialization spread to other countries, including Belgium and France.

One of the most significant developments to come out of the Industrial Revolution was the Jacquard loom. Invented as a way to automate and mass-produce woven patterns that were fashionable at the time, it inspired the foundations of modern computer science. The Jacquard loom was not just a machine capable of advanced weaving; it was the first instance of humans communicating instructions to a machine.

It all started with the desire to have beautifully patterned silk and frustration at the labor involved.

The NEED for a BETTER LOOM

Silk was first discovered in China sometime around 2700 BCE. Silk was softer, stronger, and more luxurious than any fabric seen before. For many centuries, the Chinese guarded the secrets to silk production, and it wasn't until around 140 BCE that the methods of silk production spread to India. Hundreds of years later, the knowledge spread to Persia and eventually made its way into Europe.

Silk production made its way to France during the reign of King Louis XI, who ruled from 1461 to 1483. Louis XI lavishly compensated silk experts from Italy to come to France and build a silk business. He knew that any region that had silk became a region of prosperity, and he wanted that for France.

For much of history, humans had worn animal skins and furs, moving into plant-based fabrics around 4500 BCE when the Egyptians began using flax to produce linen. With linen came the advent of weaving, or the interweaving of perpendicular strands to create a piece of material, and the loom. Looms hold a set of strands called the **warp**, which is the basis for the weaving. One end of the warp is attached to the loom on a back beam (also called a warp beam), and the other end is fastened to a front beam (also called a cloth beam). Perpendicular threads, called the **weft**, are interlaced through the warp threads with an object called a **shuttle**.

Weavers can create patterns by using draw looms, which permit the weaver to lift up different threads with each pass of the shuttle. The draw loom was first invented in China in about 200 BCE and created beautiful silk patterns. However, it was incredibly laborious and required one person to lift the threads (usually a young drawboy) and another to operate the shuttle (usually the silk weaver).

The draw loom was an impractical tool for mass-producing woven silks. In Lyon, the silk capital of France, a weaver set out to build a better way. Joseph-Marie Jacquard, son of a master silk weaver,

The Silk Road brought silk westward to places like Persia, where it was used to make beautiful woven rugs, among other textiles.

wanted a machine that could not only automatically weave beautiful designs, but a machine that could automatically weave *different* beautiful designs based on the instructions it was given. After all, a machine that could automatically weave a single specific pattern would not be useful once that pattern fell out of style. Also, a weaver would need multiple machines to produce multiple designs.

Within France, Lyon had become the most prominent city for silk work, in large part because of the money and nobility centered within the city. Lyon was a wealthy banking city, and the royal family visited often to enjoy the warm weather and make plans to take over parts of nearby Italy. The royal family and nobility had an especially large appetite for silk, the finest fabric available. The most desired cloth was brocade, an extravagantly woven silk.

Given the size of the industry and the laborious process to make woven silks, silk weavers refined the draw loom as much as possible to make it easier and faster to produce silks. Any increase in speed could mean a big difference in their profits. However, there was only so much they could do with the draw loom, and by the eighteenth century, the manual draw loom was as good as it would ever get. For the desirable brocades, it could take a team an entire day to create 1 inch (2.5 cm) of woven fabric. A set of curtains could take months to produce, and a single wrong thread could ruin a design.

Previous Motions Toward an Automatic Loom

Joseph-Marie Jacquard didn't start out entirely from scratch in his quest to build a better, faster loom. Several other Frenchmen had attempted to create an automated loom before Jacquard, and his version was a refinement of many of their ideas.

In 1725, a Lyonnais textile worker named Basile Bouchon built what is considered to be the first industrial use of a semiautomated machine. Bouchon's father built organs (the musical instrument), and Bouchon was particularly inspired by his father's automated organs. Automated organs had cylinders with pegs that determined which notes were played as the cylinder rotated. Belgian bell ringers used the same sort of cylinder to determine which bells were rung.

To build the cylinder, the designer of the musical pattern would give a carpenter a piece of paper that showed where the pegs should be. Inspired by this method of design instruction, Bouchon put a roll of perforated paper on the loom that, combined with hooks, determined which threads lifted. It worked to some degree, but it required a human to put the papers on, and the papers would often tear.

Three years later, Bouchon's assistant, Jean-Baptiste Falcon, improved on Bouchon's design by exchanging the paper roll for pasteboard cards attached to each other in a loop, which made it easier to advance the cards. However, the cards still had to be advanced by hand.

In about 1750, Jacques Vaucanson, an inspector of French silk factories, advanced the concept even further. Vaucanson's design put the perforated cards around a perforated metal cylinder with a mechanism that automatically advanced the paper. However, the metal cylinder by nature repeated the design and limited weavers to repeating design patterns. The cylinders were expensive and hard to manufacture, and combined with the design limitations, Vaucanson's design failed to revolutionize the industry.

Jacquard's Automated Loom

Vaucanson's loom ended up in a collection called the Conservatoire des Arts et Métiers (Conservatory of Arts and Trades). At the turn of the nineteenth century, Jacquard was asked to reconstruct Vaucanson's loom. Napoleon Bonaparte had risen to power in France in 1800, and he was determined to boost France's industry to match Britain's technological growth and innovation.

Jacquard had first invented and patented a foot treadle loom that could weave small patterns into fabric, which he patented in 1800. By 1804, he patented a design that combined Vaucanson's automated machine with Falcon's loop of perforated cards. The Jacquard loom had a control device that lifted hooks, which in turn lifted warp threads while a rod pushed a weft thread underneath. The perforations in the punched cards, like Falcon's design, determined which hooks lifted threads to create the design. A weaver could input an unlimited number of instructions, and the sequence could be modified by adding or changing the order of the punch cards. Often, a chain of punched cards might be as long as two thousand cards or more. It was programming, though computers were not yet invented.

This combination was wildly successful. Not only was it automatic, it was flexible. It also wove about twenty-four times faster than the traditional weaver-drawboy pairing, and a weaver could produce about 2 feet (0.6 m) of fabric per day instead of just 1 inch (2.5 cm). To show off the complexity the loom could produce, Jacquard created a tapestry based on a painting of himself commissioned by the city of Lyon. (Jacquard had become a hero for industrializing and growing the city's famed silk industry. The city also erected a bronze statue of Jacquard in 1840.) The portrait tapestry required twenty-four thousand rows of silk thread, each controlled by a separate punch card.

When Jacquard patented his invention in 1804, the Jacquard loom was considered the most complex machine in the world.

Jacquard Victorious

In 1805, Napoleon and his wife Josephine visited Jacquard's workshop in Lyon. Napoleon had just decreed the Jacquard loom to be public property, in exchange for an annual pension of 3,000 francs for Jacquard (about $96,000 in today's money) and a royalty of 50 francs (about $1,600) for every Jacquard loom used in France for the next six years. Napoleon took a liking to Jacquard and personally encouraged the use of the Jacquard loom throughout France. By 1812, there were eleven thousand Jacquard looms in operation in France, and by 1832, there were also six hundred Jacquard looms in Britain.

Jacquard spent the next two decades helping the weavers in Lyon learn to use the Jacquard loom before retiring to the countryside. Later in life, Jacquard won

The REVOLUTIONARY LIFE of JOSEPH-MARIE JACQUARD

Joseph-Marie Jacquard was born in Lyon on July 7, 1752. Jacquard's father was a silk weaver, and like most children of silk weavers in Lyon, Jacquard didn't attend school. Instead, he helped out his father. Jacquard learned to read at age twelve from his older sister's husband.

At age twenty, Jacquard's father died and he inherited the entire estate. Jacquard continued to work as a silk weaver, but by and large he lived on his father's money. He married in 1778 and had a son in 1779. By 1783, Jacquard had blown through his father's money, and he was forced to sell off his belongings. He worked as a laborer until the French Revolution broke out in 1787.

In 1793, Jacquard and his son defended the city against the revolutionaries, who were fighting for liberty from the French monarchy. Lyon had a strong counterrevolutionary force due to the presence of royals and aristocrats who visited the city and supported the silk industry there. When the city fell, Jacquard and his son fled, took false names, and joined the revolutionary forces.

Jacquard became a revolutionary officer and was later wounded in battle; his son was killed. Jacquard's life was at a low point in 1798 when he returned from fighting to Lyon. Just a year later, however, he was at work inventing a better loom. In December of 1800, he filed for his first patent for a treadle loom that used a foot treadle to create small designs in fabrics. He showed his treadle loom at an exhibition of French industry in 1801. It generated significant interest there, and later won a bronze medal for technical achievement from the French government. Jacquard was on his way back up.

In modern looms, computer-generated files dictate when to lift the warp thread to produce a pattern.

a gold medal from the government and other national accolades for his invention.

Jacquard looms are still used today, though they have new means of power and can even integrate with computer scanners as an input source for their images.

From the LOOM to the COMPUTER

Jacquard's loom made him a wealthy, successful man and changed the weaving industry forever. And yet, it had perhaps even more of an impact on society through its influence on another industry: computer science.

Babbage and Lovelace

The punch cards that Jacquard (and those before him) used to communicate design instructions to the looms were clearly applicable to other industries. They had, after all, been inspired by the design of cylinders used to make automated organs. Meanwhile, the growth of finance and industry in the nineteenth century increased the need for business machines that could make calculations, print results, and perform other business-related tasks.

In 1821, English mathematician and Royal Astronomical Society founding member Charles Babbage began working on a series of inventions used for calculations. Inaccurate mathematical tables could mean life or death for navigating sailors, and Babbage wanted to build a machine that could automate the production of those tables to ensure accuracy.

Babbage spent eleven years working on the design for his first calculating machine, the Difference Engine. The Difference Engine was based on a mathematical principle called the "method of finite differences" and could be used to complete complicated calculations and print the results. The machine included wheels with teeth. Each tooth represented a digit 0 through 9, with the movement from 9 to 0 on one wheel moving the next wheel forward (essentially carrying the digit). A good deal of the Difference Engine only existed in his designs. Though he received £17,000 in government funding (nearly $2 million today) for the Difference Engine, Babbage eventually abandoned the machine after running into construction difficulties midway through the build. If it had been fully built, it would have weighed about 4 tons (3.6 metric tons) and stood 8 feet (2.4 m) tall.

Between 1834 and 1836, Babbage worked on the designs for a new machine he called the Analytical Engine, a more general-purpose computing engine. The Analytical Engine had a more ambitious design than the Difference Engine: it was meant to carry out sequences of linked arithmetic and algebraic operations.

In design, the machine was a precursor to the modern computer. It had input and output units, a control unit, a memory (the machine could store up to one thousand numbers), a processing unit (which did the arithmetic), and a printing device. It had **conditional branching** (the ability to follow different instructions based on the value of preliminary data) and **loops** (a sequence of instructions that repeated a specified number of times or until a certain condition was met), two concepts of modern computer programming. It was programmed through punch cards, directly inspired by the Jacquard loom. This made it more versatile than any earlier calculating machine.

In 1833, Babbage showed an unfinished prototype of his machine to the teenage daughter of the poet Lord Byron, Ada Lovelace. Lovelace was an avid mathematician—her mother had insisted she be taught mathematics, in fact, to quash any poetic urges she might have inherited from her father. (The Byrons had a troubled marriage that ended shortly after Ada was born.)

Lovelace was fascinated by Babbage's work, and the two struck up a correspondence. When an Italian mathematician, Luigi Federico Menabrea, published a paper on the machine in French, Lovelace published a translation with nearly twenty thousand words of notes that became more famous than Menabrea's original paper.

In the notes, Lovelace described the device's foundations in the Jacquard loom and how the punch cards could program the machine. Lovelace's notes included descriptions of different computer programs the Analytical Engine could perform, how the machine would process those calculations, and the codes that would tell the machine how to do it. In creating instructions from start to finish that allowed a machine to reach an end result without any calculation from a human (unlike an abacus, which simply tracked the results of a human calculation), Lovelace became the first computer programmer in history.

The Birth of Punch Card Computers

Babbage ran into construction difficulties yet again and never built the machine to run Lovelace's programs, but his designs were influential on the future of computer science. In 1889, the United States Census Bureau ran a competition for a better way to gather and analyze data about the booming United States population. The winning design came from Herman Hollerith, who had invented a statistics machine that could count units electronically with punched cards. When a current passed through a punched hole, it moved a counter up one unit, tallying data such as male, female, Roman Catholic, and married. He had made real the computer concept that Babbage designed, though for a different purpose.

Hollerith later went on to found the Tabulating Machine Co. in 1896. In 1924, the corporation changed its name to the International Business Machines Corp., or IBM.

IBM turned punch card technology into many products, selling both the punch cards themselves and tabulators that combined electrical circuitry, machinery, and punch cards to process data. Decades later, IBM would become a computer giant.

Hollerith and others continued to improve on punch cards and created a worldwide information-processing industry. Punch cards survived until the 1970s as a means of communicating data to computers. They were eventually replaced by electronic computers.

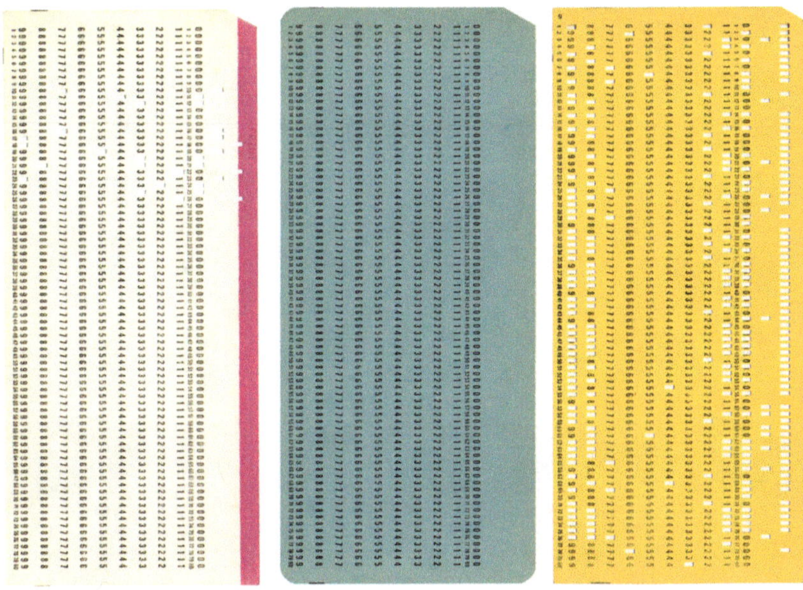

Colored punch cards allowed programmers to color-code their decks based on card function; the diagonal cut indicated which way to insert the card.

Toy Story included about 1,700 shots and 76 characters carefully modeled, detailed, and animated using computer graphics software.

CHAPTER 4
BEFLIX and the First Computer Animations

In the 1930s, academics began building more technologically advanced computers. An engineer at the Massachussets Institute of Technology, Vannevar Bush, built the first modern analog computer. Bush's computer, called the Differential Analyzer, was designed to solve differential equations. At Harvard, Howard Aiken built a series of calculating machines that progressed from a mechanical version (the Mark I) to an electronic version (the Mark IV). The Mark I–Mark IV could read both punch cards and paper tape.

In the 1940s, computer science progressed to electronic machines, computer networks, and stored programs. In the 1950s and 60s, computer scientists began to write high-level programming languages, including FORTRAN and COBOL, that could be translated into the binary code that machines understand. These new languages made programming more accessible to more people. They looked more like mathematics or English and were therefore easier to write and understand than binary code. (At first, the written programs were still converted into punch cards.)

Many more innovations and changes occurred in the design, programming, and use of computers beyond the scope of this book, but overall, the trend in the middle of the twentieth century was to build increasingly fast, powerful, and flexible machines.

The ENIGMA and the COLOSSUS: A BRIDGE BETWEEN EARLY and MODERN COMPUTING

As warfare grew increasingly technological, military needs drove many advancements in computing. The need to decrypt German intelligence led to the development of the first fully electronic, digital, binary computer.

After World War I, German leaders began looking for a system that would allow them to communicate quickly and securely with their troops. They turned to the Enigma machine. The Enigma (Greek for "riddle") was a portable device that scrambled typed messages using three mechanical rotating wheels (rotors) that substituted different letters of the alphabet for the original message. Each key press advanced at least one wheel to create a different substitution alphabet after every keystroke. The recipient entered the encrypted text into a second Enigma machine with the same settings, which reversed the encryption.

The German military used the Enigma machines during World War II to encrypt messages sent on the battlefields, to ships, and within their secret service. The messages included important information such as the deployment of U-boats that were attacking the British forces, which made the messages immensely valuable to the Allies.

To crack the Enigma code, the British government tucked a team of top mathematicians and decryption experts away at Bletchley Park, made up of outbuildings on the grounds of a Victorian manor house. The computer scientist Alan Turing led the first project, building a decryption machine called the "bombe" that was ready in 1940. The bombe was an **electromechanical** machine (or a mechanical device that is electrically operated). It had rotors and **relay switches** and cracked the Enigma code by using known weaknesses in the code, such as the fact that certain phrases were frequently repeated. Turing's bombe helped crack hundreds of messages, including some that helped British admiral Andrew Cunningham defeat the Italian navy in an important battle off the coast of Greece.

At the end of the war, the Allied forces paid a $7,500 bounty for Enigma machines and destroyed those that were not displayed in museums. The machines had been so effective that they were considered a future danger, even after the code had been broken.

The highest officers in Hitler's command later turned to an even more powerful device, the Lorenz SZ-40. The Lorenz machine had twelve cipher wheels of different sizes that sent messages in code. It was so much more advanced than the Enigma codes that the Allied forces needed something much faster and more powerful than Turing's bombes.

Tommy Flowers, an electronics engineer and bombe-team veteran, built the Colossus, a machine that could read punched paper tapes at an astonishing rate. It could also electronically generate the wheel patterns of the Lorenz machine. Flowers built the machine at the Post Office Research Station in North West London and had it delivered to Bletchley Park in January of 1944. The machine's decryptions included messages confirming that Hitler wasn't deploying extra troops to Normandy, a reassuring message for General Dwight Eisenhower who was about to launch the D-Day invasion.

The Colossus machine is considered the first fully electronic, digital, binary computer, but it was a computer designed specifically for code breaking. The ENIAC computer, built from 1943 to 1945, would be the first fully electronic, digital, binary, general-purpose computer.

Like the Enigma machines, most Colossus computers were destroyed after the war.

The Colossus did not store programs and, like the ENIAC, was reprogrammed for different jobs by modifying the machine's wiring. The version here is a reconstruction.

Computers were still very large and expensive, and most computers belonged to universities or corporate research and development teams. One of those teams was Bell Labs, a subsidiary of AT&T and a center of innovation. Scientists at Bell Labs invented the **transistor** (a semiconductor device used today in computer memory chips), developed the first satellite communication system, and discovered the cosmic microwave background radiation left over from the Big Bang. In the 1960s, a computer scientist at Bell Labs built the first programming language for film animation.

A REVOLUTION in FILM ANIMATION

The first computer graphics were invented as ways to monitor what was happening within the computer's memory operations. Soon, displays were used to track missile trajectories and, by 1963, airplanes. At the same time, early computer games began to appear, such as *Spacewar!* from a team at the Massachusetts Institute of Technology.

At Bell Labs, a computer scientist saw another application for the fledgling computer graphics industry. Before computer animation, animated movies were produced in a slow, heavily hands-on process. Kenneth Knowlton saw an opportunity to use computers to change that process forever.

Traditional Animation

In traditional animation, an illustrator draws a series of images with small changes such that, frame by frame, the drawings represent a sequence over time.

For example, to create an animated sequence of a woman chopping wood, the illustrator would create a series of drawings with her arm holding the ax in a number of positions. To create the illusion of an object moving, different characters and objects in a scene are inked and painted on transparent sheets of celluloid (called **cels**). When the woman is holding the ax, she and the ax could be painted on the same cel. When she puts the ax down, they would be painted on separate cels so she could be made to move independently of the ax.

The cels are stacked on top of each other with the background layer (or layers) at the bottom and photographed. Between shots, someone moves the background and cels to advance the story. A movie camera would capture the sequence of images on film and create the effect of animation. For many traditionally animated movies, twelve drawings per second are shown, except in scenes with quick movements, when the rate increases to twenty-four drawings per second to create a more lifelike effect.

Computer Animation's Beginnings

Kenneth Knowlton, a computer scientist at Bell Labs, wanted to create a way to produce animated films on computers. He wrote to his department head and suggested that a programming language could transform the process of making animated movies. The department head gave him permission to work on the project.

In 1963, Knowlton developed BEFLIX, which stands for Bell Flicks. The programming language could create and manipulate pictures using **pixels** (minute areas of a display screen) and **bitmaps** (a file that indicates the color, pixel by pixel, of regions on a display screen). Each picture was made of a number of small square pixels in shades of gray, which could be used to create what Knowlton called "mosaics."

The programmer or artist animated the picture by altering the pattern of shaded squares to create the perception of motion or change.

BEFLIX, which Knowlton called a "movie language," could draw straight and curved lines, draw circles and arcs, type words, paint shapes, shift and grow shapes, and more. Instructions for the movie would be entered into a computer on punch cards (such as "Paint," "Center," "Place") and the computer would create the movie frame by frame. The descriptions of the images were written on magnetic tape that controlled the camera and display tube. The resulting film was processed like normal photographs.

"The speed, ease, and economy of computer animation permits the movie-maker to take several tries at a scene—producing a whole family of film clips—from which he chooses the most appealing result, a luxury never before possible," Knowlton wrote.

COMPUTER ANIMATION ADVANCEMENTS

In 1968, an artist named Lillian Schwartz joined Bell Labs as an artist in residence. Schwartz began her career as a pen-and-ink artist who moved into oil and acrylics and then plastic paintings and collages.

Schwartz met Kenneth Knowlton in 1968 at the Machine Exhibition at the Museum of Modern Art (MoMA). It was there she first encountered computer art. She had a sculpture called *Proxima Centauri* in the exhibition that observers could interact with by stepping on a pad that generated effects on the sculpture's globe.

Kenneth Knowlton and his coworker Leon Harmon had created a 12-foot- (3.6 m) wide graphic called *Study in Perception* that used computer symbols to create a large gray-scale image of a reclining woman. Knowlton and Harmon had hung the graphic in a coworker's office when he was away and the piece eventually became famous outside of Bell Labs, appearing in the *New York Times* in 1967 before making it to the MoMA.

After the art exhibition, Harmon invited Schwartz to Bell Labs, where she became a consultant and resident artist. At Bell Labs, Schwartz propelled the development of computer-animated movies forward. She wanted more control over the pixels throughout the entire process than Knowlton's first movie language, BEFLIX, allowed.

Schwartz collaborated with Knowlton to produce his next computer animation programming language, EXPLOR (which stands for EXplicit Patterns, Local Operations and Randomness). The result was much different than the simple lines and shading of BEFLIX. EXPLOR allowed an artist to scan an image and create patterns with it.

Schwartz created a number of films using EXPLOR, including *Pixallation* in 1970. The four-minute film won the Cine Golden Eagle Award in 1971, which recognizes excellence in the film, television, and digital media industry. That same year, the MoMA acquired the film. She also used EXPLOR to create the first animated running man to have anatomically correct joints in her film *Olympiad.*

KNOWLTON and SCHWARTZ

Kenneth Knowlton was born in Springville, New York, in 1931 and graduated from Cornell in 1953 with a bachelor's degree in physics and again in 1955 with a master's degree in physics. He went on to receive a PhD in computer science from the Massachusetts Institute of Technology in 1962. He spent twenty years working at Bell Labs.

While at Bell Labs, Knowlton collaborated with numerous artists, including Lillian Schwartz and Stan VanDerBeek. VanDerBeek used Knowlton's BEFLIX to turn his poetry into geometric, animated graphics. After inventing BEFLIX and EXPLOR, Knowlton took a year off from Bell Labs to teach computer graphics at the University of California, Santa Cruz.

Between 1968 and 2002, Knowlton had artwork in dozens of shows. After leaving Bell Labs, Knowlton reversed the computer-centric focus of his art and worked on increasingly analog artwork. His focus in later years turned to mosaic portraits.

While Knowlton started as a scientist and became progressively identified more as an artist, Lillian Schwartz was an artist from a young age. She was born in 1927 to a family of thirteen children. She drew and sketched extensively. While serving as a nurse in the army, Schwartz began to make sculptures out of plaster before moving to make more dynamic sculptures out of whatever electronics she could find.

She later moved to Japan to join her husband. While there, she contracted polio. During recovery, as she struggled with paralysis from the disease, she learned Chinese brushwork.

After becoming an artist in residence at Bell Labs, Schwartz established the computer as a medium for animated films and special effects. In 1985, she created the first computer-generated public service announcement, commissioned by the Museum of Modern Art, which went on to become the first computer-animated PSA to win an Emmy Award.

COMMERCIAL COMPUTER ANIMATIONS

BEFLIX and EXPLOR didn't remain the standards of computer animation programming, but they kicked off an era of innovation that is still going strong today.

In 1974, the founder of the New York Institute of Technology (NYIT), Alexander Schure, established a Computer Graphics Lab. Schure wanted to create a feature-length animated film, and he stocked the lab with the best computers and recruited top talent to realize his dream.

"He viewed us as the artists of the future, as the new animators," said the lab's founding director, Ed Catmull. Other founding team members included Alvy Ray Smith and David DiFrancesco, two former employees of Xerox PARC, a pioneer in the graphical user interface (which is covered more in the next chapter).

Schure didn't realize his dream of a full-length animated film, but the NYIT team did advance the industry with full-color graphics, the first full-color paint program, the first computer-controlled video editing, and more.

In 1979, George Lucas, director of *Star Wars*, recruited Catmull to build machines, including a digital film editor, a digital sound editor, and a digital film printer. Many of his team members from the NYIT followed, including Alvy Ray Smith. With the financial help of an investor, Steve Jobs, the same group that had moved from the NYIT to Lucasfilm formed Pixar in 1986.

By the early 1990s, computer animation began to appear in films like *Beauty and the Beast* and *Terminator 2*. *Beauty and the Beast* was the second film to use the Computer Animation Production System (CAPS) that Pixar built for Disney. CAPS included software and hardware for creating colors and shading, layering (a computer technique much like the layering of cel sheets in traditional animation), simulating depth (again using computers to simulate the layered backgrounds of traditional animation), and combining hand-drawn art with computer-generated imagery. Much of *Beauty and the Beast* was created using traditional animation, but the movie's famous ballroom sequence was created using the CAPS technology.

"With 'Beauty and the Beast,' a tender, seamless and even more ambitious film than its predecessor, Disney has done something no one has done before: combine the latest computer animation techniques with the best of Broadway," the *New York Times* wrote in its review of the film. For the computer-animated ballroom scene and the soundtrack's accompanying love song, "the viewer would be well advised to bring a hanky," the reviewer wrote. The computer, it seemed, was capable of producing art as emotionally provoking as the human hand.

In 1995, Pixar (with Steve Jobs as its chairman) produced the first full-length computer animated film: *Toy Story.* It was a huge success, bringing in over $361 million worldwide and becoming the first animated film to receive Academy Award nominations for Best Original Song, Best Score, and Best Screenplay.

The film's cowriter, director, and animation team leader John Lasseter won a Special Achievement Academy Award for his work. Ed Catmull, Alvy Ray Smith, and two other founding members of Pixar, Thomas Porter and Tom Duff, received the Scientific and Engineering Academy Award for their work in digital image composing. Since *Toy Story*, hundreds of computer animated feature films have been released, including several *Toy Story* sequels.

Advancements in Computing

When Kenneth Knowlton first invented BEFLIX and later EXPLOR with Lillian Schwartz, the resulting animations were simple compared to what we're used to today. Nonetheless, they were the first instances of using computers to animate films. Computer animation has become the standard for animated films today. Its widespread use and commercial success depended on huge advancements in personal computing and computer graphics. Many of these advancements were pioneered by the tech giant Apple.

The Apple II came with just four kilobytes of RAM (computer memory), compared to the gigabytes of RAM that come in modern PCs.

CHAPTER 5
The Apple Computer

Two men invented the first Apple computer. One, Steve Jobs, was an artist, technician, and entrepreneur. The other, Steve Wozniak, was a gifted programmer and electronics guru. The two men both attended Homestead High School in Cupertino, California, and were introduced by a mutual friend because both Steves loved electronics and practical jokes. Years after they met, Jobs and Wozniak built the first Apple computers and, in bringing personal computers to a consumer audience, began a computer revolution.

Wozniak led much of the technical work behind the early Apple products, while Jobs, a self-identified artist, focused on design and entrepreneurship.

JOBS the ARTIST

Steve Jobs grew up working on shop projects with his father, Paul. Jobs loved electronics but was also passionate about art and design. In high school, he loved music, literature, and poetry. While many of his Silicon Valley–raised classmates went to college at Stanford, Jobs enrolled at the liberal arts institution Reed College in Portland, Oregon, in hopes of finding an artistic and interesting college experience.

Jobs dropped out of Reed College, but his experience there shaped his later career. Notably, after dropping out, he audited a class in calligraphy that introduced him to typography, including serif and sans serif fonts and letter spacing. "It was beautiful, historical, artistically subtle in a way that science can't capture, and I found it fascinating," Jobs said at a commencement address he later gave at—ironically—Stanford University. "If I had never dropped out, I would have never dropped in on this calligraphy class, and personal computers might not have the wonderful typography that they do."

Apple's Beginnings

After Jobs's experience at Reed—followed by a trip to India—he returned to California. Wozniak worked at Hewlett Packard and had joined the Homebrew Computer Club, a group founded in 1975 as a way for computer enthusiasts to share knowledge and parts and make computers more accessible.

At the time, few ordinary people owned a computer because they were large, expensive, and not particularly user friendly. Those who had computers typically built them from scratch, which created a huge barrier to use for anyone who wasn't good at computer science.

The first affordable, assembled computer aimed at the general public was the Altair 8800, which launched in March of 1975 and sold for $621. The Altair 8800 didn't come with a keyboard or monitor, however, and users had to enter programs using switches on the front panel of the computer and watch for flashing lights that showed the program results.

The first Homebrew meeting featured the Altair. At the meeting, Wozniak saw a specification sheet for the Intel **microprocessor** inside the Altair and, as he reviewed the technical details, a vision popped into his head: an all-in-one computer with both a keyboard and monitor. Just a few months later, in June of 1975,

The success of Apple's computers and other digital products helped Steve Jobs accumulate an estimated $8.3 billion in wealth.

The Apple III had no fans or vents and grew disruptively hot when it ran. Sales were poor.

Wozniak had built the Apple I, a fully assembled **circuit** board. (Users had to add a case, keyboard and display, among other components, to make the Apple I a fully working computer.) Wozniak wanted to give the computer away for free, but Jobs pushed to monetize Wozniak's creation. The two founded Apple Computer in 1977. They quickly improved on their first, bare-bones computer to create the Apple II, a no-assembly-required personal computer.

With its accessible design, the Apple II was much more suitable to a mass market than previous personal computers. They also advertised to a very different market, including running ads in popular magazines instead of in the technical journals where other computer companies of the time advertised. In various models, Apple sold nearly six million Apple IIs and effectively launched the personal computer industry. It still had a text-based interface, however, which limited its artistic potential.

The MACINTOSH and iMAC

In 1984, Apple launched the Macintosh as the first commercially available personal computer with a graphical user interface, the image-based computer interface we know today. Again, Apple had revolutionized the computer industry.

The Birth of the Macintosh

The graphical user interface (GUI) grew out of a research center named Xerox PARC (part of the Xerox copy machine company), which was refining bitmapping in the 1970s. Bitmapping uses a grid of pixels (picture elements) to map information to regions on a display screen, and the method allowed computer programmers and designers to create an interface with images and fonts. The result completely changed the look and feel of computers.

In 1979, Jobs and a team of Apple employees went to Xerox PARC for a demo of the technology behind the GUI in exchange for a deal on Apple stock. Jobs and his team took what they learned, improved on it, and incorporated the GUI into the design of two personal computers released a few years later.

The first to be released, the Lisa computer in 1983, was a commercial failure. The Lisa computer had a graphics-based desktop, but it cost $9,995 and was too expensive for a general audience. (That's the equivalent of over $24,000 today.) Sales of the Lisa were slow, and by 1985 the product line was discontinued.

In January of 1984, Apple released the Macintosh computer, which sold for $2,495. Like the Lisa, the Macintosh had graphical icons, including a wastebasket and files and folders, that could be dragged and dropped using a mouse. These simple, familiar elements were completely revolutionary at the time for users who were used to typing commands to control their computer.

Steven Levy, who covered the launch of the Macintosh for *Rolling Stone*, later recalled his first introduction to the Macintosh:

> Until that point, personal computers were locked in an esoteric realm of codes and commands. They looked unfriendly, with the letters of text growing in sickly phosphorescence … For the first time, ordinary people had the power to format text as professional printers did.

The Macintosh sold well at first, and then, in part due to the limited number of applications, sales slumped. It had just two programs: MacWrite, a word processing tool, and MacPaint, a drawing tool. Despite its limitations, however, many felt that the Macintosh looked like the future of computers.

After adding new programs and enhanced memory capabilities, Apple was again trailblazing new frontiers. The Apple II and Apple's Macintosh, as well as improved computer graphics software such as Adobe Photoshop, allowed computer users to manipulate images and create sophisticated designs. The advancements effectively changed many industries, from publishing to photography to graphic design. Creative work that was once done on older technology such as typewriters, by hand, or by large publishing companies who had access to fonts and printing presses could now be done at home on an affordable computer.

Apple sold one million Macintoshes in 1987 and was back in the game. Steve Jobs, however, was out. He had a challenging leadership style, a strained relationship with the CEO he had recruited, and the initially poor Macintosh sales under his belt. Apple's board removed Jobs's responsibilities and moved him to a far-flung office. Jobs left.

The Birth of the iMac

Apple struggled without its visionary leader. Meanwhile, Jobs founded a computer company called NeXT and later bought Pixar from Lucasfilm. In 1996, Apple acquired NeXT, and in a rather unexpected turn of events, Jobs was back at the helm of Apple. By 1997, he was CEO of the company he had founded with Steve Wozniak twenty years earlier with a big task ahead of him: Jobs had to turn the now-struggling computer company around.

He did so by focusing on four major products, specifically one desktop and one portable (laptop) computer

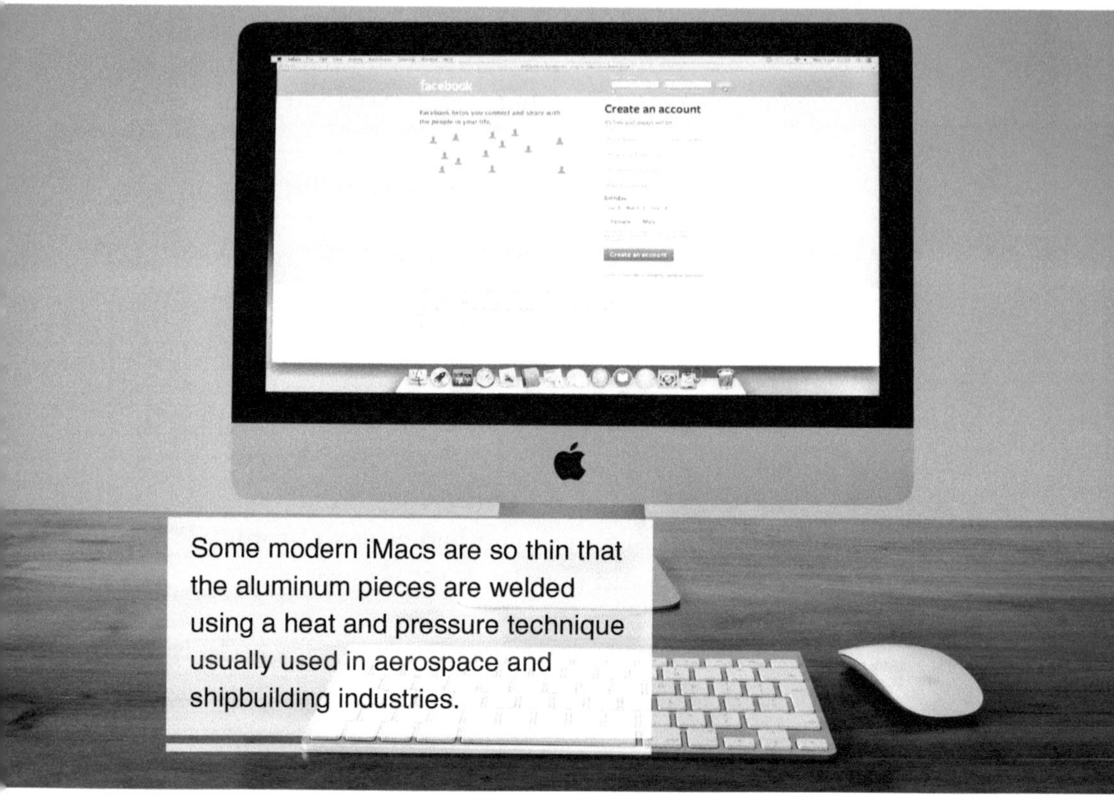

Some modern iMacs are so thin that the aluminum pieces are welded using a heat and pressure technique usually used in aerospace and shipbuilding industries.

each for the consumer and pro markets. In the consumer desktop category was the latest version of the Macintosh, the iMac.

Jobs worked closely with Apple's lead designer, Jony Ive, on the design for the iMac. When it launched in 1998, it was a sleek, curved, all-in-one computer with a transparent blue case. It was friendly and accessible to anyone who had previously avoided computers, and it became the fastest-selling computer in Apple's history.

Its success didn't have much immediate effect on Job's personal fortune, as he took a $1-per-year salary in his first years back at Apple, with no stock options. However, Jobs later negotiated for a private jet and $20 million in stock options.

The PASSION of STEVE JOBS

"I'm convinced that the only thing that kept me going was that I loved what I did. You've got to find what you love … Your work is going to fill a large part of your life, and the only way to be truly satisfied is to do what you believe is great work."

—Steve Jobs in a 2005 Stanford commencement address

Steve Jobs has many legacies. He is known for being the business brain who pushed to monetize Apple's first products and build a business around them. He is known for being a challenging leader who could be difficult, even cruel. And he is known for being a revolutionary designer who changed the way our devices look today. Above all, he was passionate about what he did.

When he saw beautifully drawn posters on the campus of Reed College, he attended calligraphy classes to learn how they were made. His interest in meditation led him on a seven-month spiritual quest in India in 1974. A drive for health inspired him to keep a strict vegan, at times fruitarian diet (eating only parts of the plant that allow the plant to keep growing).

Even when he was pushed out of the company he founded, he founded a new company (NeXT) and kept building beautiful (if buggy) computers. By pursuing what he loved so much, he ended up right back at Apple. At the helm for the second time, Jobs threw himself into creating the next generation of the Macintosh and the succession of i-devices, and built Apple into one of the most valuable public company in the world.

Jobs died in October 2011, at the age of fifty-six, due to pancreatic cancer.

iPODS, iTUNES, iPHONES, and ART

After Jobs returned, he propelled Apple through a series of new inventions that sold like wildfire and forever changed the music, photography, and communications industries.

iTunes

In January 2001 at the Macworld conference in San Francisco, Jobs heralded the arrival of what he called the "Digital Lifestyle" with the Mac at its center. It would be the "digital hub" for a booming digital devices industry. In this talk, Jobs introduced iTunes, a digital music library with an emphasis on simplicity and power. Other media players existed, such as Windows Media Player, but they were complex and came with restrictions on quality and speed. "We're late to this party and we're going to do a leapfrog," Jobs told the audience.

iTunes allowed users to build a music library by ripping CDs (compact discs), creating playlists, and burning their own CDs from their library. In October of that same year, Apple launched the iPod, a portable music player. In 2001 and 2002 alone, Apple sold 600,000 iPods. By 2010, Apple had sold over 275 million iPods.

In 2003, Apple launched the iTunes Music Store, a digital marketplace for music where songs cost ninety-nine cents each and albums cost ten dollars. Within one week, Apple had sold one million songs. The music industry changed forever.

In 2000, before digital music was of any significance, Americans bought almost 1 billion CD albums. By 2007, digital singles outsold CDs by 819 million sales to 500 million sales. It was now possible to pick and choose individual songs instead of buying a whole album. By 2008, the iTunes Store had become the United States' largest music retailer, ahead of Walmart, Best Buy, and Amazon. By 2013, consumers had downloaded over 25 billion songs on iTunes.

As the iTunes Store's profits rose, the music industry faced big challenges. Between 2003 and 2010, debut album sales fell 77 percent globally, according to the International Federation of the Phonographic Industry. As album sales declined and single-track sales rose, musicians had to find new ways to make money, often through touring and merchandise sales.

It wasn't iTunes that brought about the decrease in album sales, however. Other services had been illegally sharing digital music for years, and iTunes was the first digital marketplace to effectively compete with pirated music. According to Sony Music Entertainment CEO Doug Morris in an interview with *Billboard*, "Some people say Apple unbundled the album. In my mind, it had already been unbundled by piracy. So why not do it in a way in which we get paid? That's what iTunes really did."

The iPhone

In January of 2007, Apple entered the mobile phone market with the iPhone. The iPhone had the classic elements of Jobs's design sensibility, including simplicity and ease of use. It also had a camera that became so good over subsequent versions that in 2011 the professional photographer Annie Leibovitz recommended that people buy an iPhone for point-and-shoot photography.

"That is the snapshot camera of today," she told NBC Nightly News. "It's so accessible and easy."

Accessibility and ease define the creative power of the iPhone. The camera is available instantly and produces high-quality pictures. Paired with apps like Instagram, it's easy to take, edit, and share photos of aesthetically pleasing meals, vacations, and a never-ending stream of cats.

The iPhone and Apple's tablet, the iPad, opened up other digital art forms as well. Between 2009 and 2010, artist Jorge Colombo created landscapes of New York City that appeared on covers of the *New Yorker* magazine and later in a book called *New York: Finger Paintings*. They were indeed finger paintings, in a loose sense of the term: Colombo's canvas was an iPhone. According to Colombo:

> Until the iPhone/iPad touch-screen boom, painting digitally was for the most part an indoor affair. On a park bench, even a laptop felt clumsy, let alone one with a drawing tablet connected to it. The iPhone/Brushes combo turned out to be to digital painting what 35mm film and Leica cameras were to early photography.

Colombo used an original version of the Brushes application, built by former Apple software engineer Steve Sprang.

Apple's Financial Success

After the return of Jobs and the launch of the iMac, iPods, iPhones, and iPads, Apple experienced enormous financial success. Apple had gone public in 1980 and raised around $100 million with stock shares value at $2.75 per share. By 1983, the company had annual revenue of nearly $1 billion and a stock price of almost $8 per share. The value of Apple stock suffered significantly after Jobs left and was at less than $4 per share when Jobs returned in 1996. Jobs propelled the company through enormous growth in the next fifteen years, which saw the launch of the iMac, the iPod, the iPhone, and the iPad. In 2011, when Jobs resigned, the company had annual revenue of $100 billion, a stock price of about $380 per share, and a market value of $360 billion.

In August of 2012, Apple was valued at $623.5 billion and was the world's most valuable public company. (Its value has since fallen to about $529.3 billion in 2016.)

JOBS'S DESIGN REVOLUTION

Many of Apple's products were not the first of their kind. There was a personal computer before the Macintosh; there were MP3 players and smartphones before the iPod and iPhone. Yet there is no question that each product forever changed the industry it entered. What Apple brought to the table was not necessarily first-of-its-kind innovation. Rather, it was Steve Jobs's focus on clean, simple, and top-quality design that took those products and made them more beautiful and easy to use than any product ever before.

Jobs was an entrepreneur and a technician, but what separated him from every other entrepreneur and technician was his lifelong pursuit of art and the place where that art and technology could find harmony.

Oculus Rift started in 2012 as a do-it-yourself kit. It finally shipped in 2016 as an assembled headset.

CHAPTER 6
The Future of Art and Computing

From virtual reality to 3D printing, there are numerous new ways to create art and to merge art and technology. Often, as seen in the case of computers, new technology is expensive and limited to government, academic, and business use. As the cost of these new technologies comes down, artists and the wider consumer audience gain access to the tools, and they change the way art is created and shared.

ART in VIRTUAL REALITY

Virtual reality, or the immersion into a three-dimensional, computer-generated environment, is one of the big buzzwords in industries from tech to automotives. The military uses virtual reality (VR) to realistically (but safely) prepare soldiers for combat or to work in dangerous settings. The *New York Times* built an app that, when paired with an inexpensive VR viewer, immerses readers in 360-degree settings around the world, such as the United States presidential campaign trail or candlelight vigils in Paris after the November 2015 terrorist attacks. Car companies use virtual reality as a way to give customers a virtual test drive, and surgeons use VR to practice highly technical surgeries before operating on flesh-and-blood patients.

VR has been in existence for decades. Starting in the 1950s, in the era of room-sized computers without GUIs, computer science visionaries like Douglas Engelbart saw the future of computers that displayed digital information and reduced barriers between human and machine. Engelbart later went on to build the first computer mouse to allow humans to move text around on the screen, a step forward for human movement in a virtual environment.

The flight simulator, however, was one of the most influential early advancements in VR. The military spent millions of dollars on technology to simulate flying, as well as driving tanks and piloting ships. It was cheaper and safer to train pilots in virtual environments. At first, the flight simulators didn't have visual elements, but eventually the virtual cockpits were paired with video displays and later, in the 1970s, computer-generated graphics. By the 1980s, the state of technology from software to hardware had improved such that pilots could virtually train in highly detailed, computer-generated worlds.

Nintendo and Sega built VR headsets for gaming in the 1990s, but they weren't particularly user friendly and left people physically ill after playing. When the internet went big in the 1990s, VR was temporarily set aside.

Two decades later, the Oculus Rift VR headset has brought VR back to the forefront of the tech world. The Oculus Rift was created by Palmer Luckey, who was sixteen when he started making VR headsets and nineteen when he started his company, Oculus VR. In 2014, at twenty-one, Luckey sold Oculus to Facebook for $2 billion. The Rift provides the best yet experience of VR and has movement sensors, positional sensors, 3D graphics, vibrations, audio, and more to create a high-resolution immersive experience. When Facebook bought Oculus, it showed CEO Mark Zuckerberg's faith in the future of VR. "One day, we believe this kind of immersive,

augmented reality will become a part of daily life for billions of people," Zuckerberg wrote in a Facebook post. "By feeling truly present, you can share unbounded spaces and experiences with the people in your life."

Google released an inexpensive cardboard device that turns smartphones into VR devices and has launched a more ambitious VR division. Microsoft has built an augmented reality device called the HoloLens, not yet released at the time of writing, that layers holographic images over real world views.

According to *Fortune* magazine, the market for VR by 2020 may be $150 billion. There are huge tech companies behind VR and huge amounts of money in it—and many artists are starting to explore the impact it will have on the art world.

Visual Art in VR

Virtual reality allows artists who traditionally use pencils, paint, paper, and clay to turn their two-dimensional art into three-dimensional creations.

In April 2015, Google bought an app called Tilt Brush that allows artists to use VR to paint the three-dimensional space around them. To paint, artists wearing an HTC Vive VR headset select colors and brushes and move their hands to simulate painting. The users can move around, inside of, and through their paintings, and can use materials otherwise unavailable to artists, such as fire, snowflakes, or light.

"It is more like clay and using stripes of clay to lay over a surface. I got very good at hand-eye coordination after a while," said painter Tim O'Brien after using Tilt Brush. "It didn't take long before you actually started thinking that way, instead of 2D, you thought 3D." (O'Brien's work has been commissioned by the organizations including the United States Postal Service and *Time* magazine and appears in the National Gallery of Art.)

In addition to apps like Tilt Brush that make 3D art available to anyone who can access the equipment, other artists are more heavily involved in programming their own VR environments. One such programmer and artist is Rachel Rossin, whose works include a piece called *n=7 / The Wake in Heat of Collapse* in which viewers navigate a three-dimensional, multilevel underworld filled with images from Picasso's *Guernica* and Gustav Klimt's *The Kiss*, as well as pop-up ads and brand logos. Each level unpredictably collapses, dropping the viewer into a new level with new imagery.

3D-PRINTED ART and FASHION

Today's 3D printers work like the familiar inkjet printers that put tiny bits of ink down on paper, except 3D printers deposit materials such as plastic or metals in layers. This process creates a three-dimensional object instead of a two-dimensional printout.

The first 3D printer was invented in the 1980s when Charles Hull, founder of 3D Systems, invented stereolithography. This printing process used an ultraviolet (UV) laser to trace a design on UV-sensitive **polymers** and solidify them, layer by layer, into a 3D object. The design instructions came from a digital computer-aided design (CAD) file, which is still the standard file used today. Stereolithography was an expensive technique—machines cost as much as $100,000 or more.

In the 1990s, 3D printing continued to advance as scientists used the technology to print the support structure for lab-grown organs. For many years, however, the printers were too expensive to become widely popular. It wasn't until the mid-2000s that the technology started to become

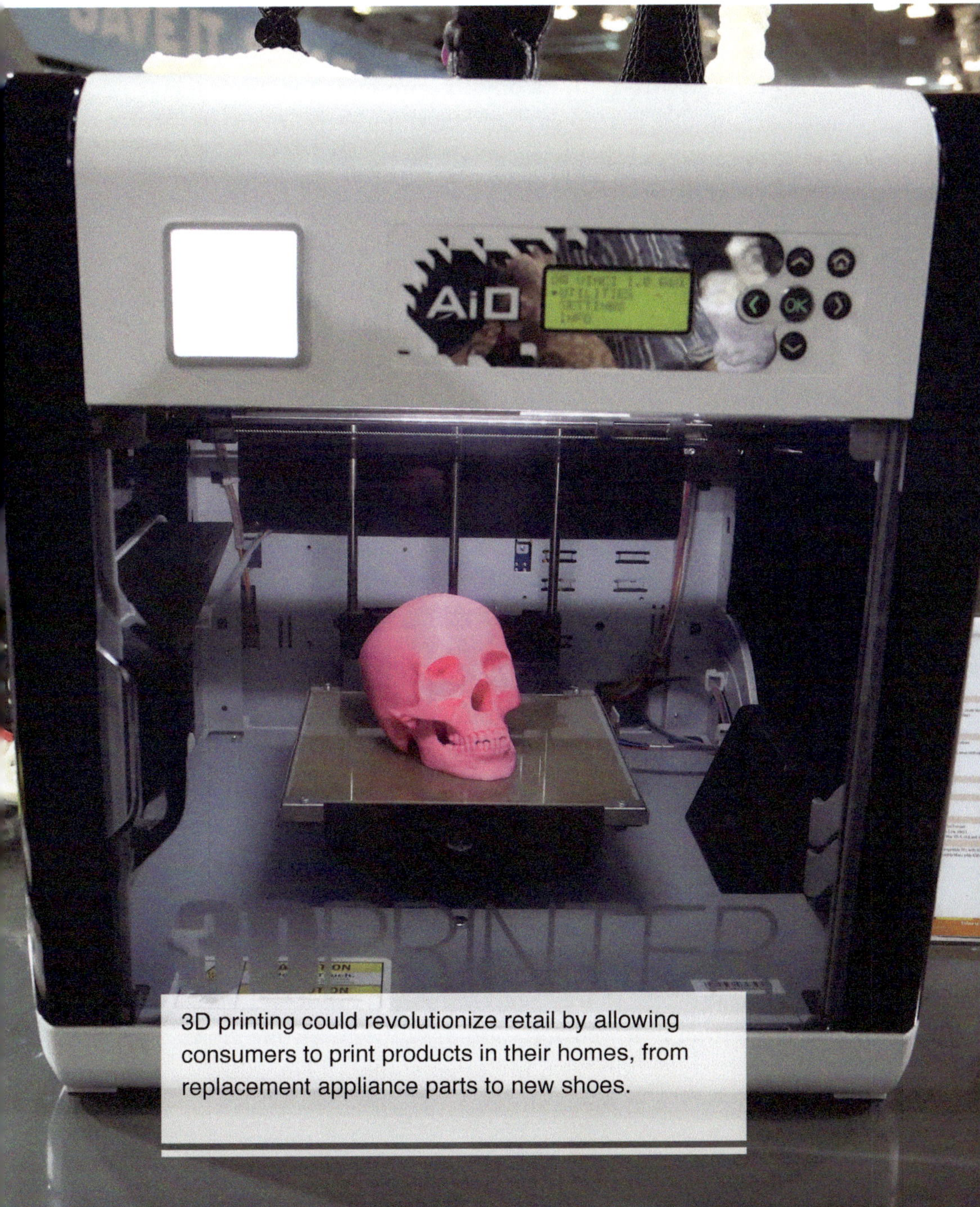

3D printing could revolutionize retail by allowing consumers to print products in their homes, from replacement appliance parts to new shoes.

both more sophisticated and more accessible. Today, there are many different types of 3D printers that that can take a CAD file and turn it into a physical product. Some printers use lasers to fuse materials together, some extrude strings of melted material that harden into layers, and some spray thin layers of photopolymers, while others combine liquid binding agents with powdered materials to produce the desired design.

In 2008, Shapeways launched a service that allowed artists and designers to upload their 3D designs and order prints, much like a photographer might order two-dimensional prints of their film from a photo printing service. In 2011, 3D printing in gold and silver became available, which opened up a new manufacturing process for jewelry designers working with those materials. Today, companies including Staples and the United Parcel Service offer 3D printing services. Many makerspaces include 3D printers that members can use, and the price for a low-end 3D printer has fallen below $1,000. This low price makes them accessible for individuals to own as well.

"We don't exist in an economy right now where the metal smith is particularly valuable, so here we're trying to see if we can sew together the 21st century maker," said jewelry designer Joshua DeMonte, who uses 3D printing to make his jewelry. "Ultimately, there's kind of a new type of maker."

In the fashion industry, 3D printing is also growing in prominence. Designer Iris van Herpen pioneered the use of 3D printing in high-end fashion in 2011, and other designers have followed suit. Some print entire collections, such as the collection fashion design student Dani Peleg produced for her graduation project from Shenkar, an engineering, design, and art school in Israel. Others incorporate 3D printing into their designs, such as the fashion house Pringle of Scotland. Pringle of Scotland,

Young, independent designers and fashion powerhouses like Chanel are turning to 3D printing to create garments.

IRIS VAN HERPEN and the 3D-PRINTED FUTURE of FASHION

In the debut of her 2010 collection "Crystallization," fashion designer Iris van Herpen sent the first 3D garment down a major fashion runway. The sculpted white top grabbed the industry's attention, and in 2011, van Herpen debuted a second collection with 3D-printed dresses at the Paris Haute Couture Fashion Week. The dresses, including a beautiful creation of crumpled white fabric, were named one of the fifty best inventions of 2011 by *Time* magazine.

Van Herpen was born in 1984 in the Netherlands. She studied fashion at the ArtEZ Institute of the Arts in the Netherlands and interned with fashion designer Alexander McQueen in London, where she gained experience working with expensive, unique materials. A year after graduating from fashion school, she began working on her own lines of women's wear.

Van Herpen pairs with scientists and technologists to inspire and produce her designs. One dress, a transparent, bell-shaped piece called "Ice," was inspired by a visit to the Large Hadron Collider at CERN in Switzerland. Another collection was inspired by the idea of terraforming (making other planets into places humans can live) and included a dress made of woven stainless steel in the colors of interstellar nebulae.

To van Herpen, 3D printing fashion is a logical choice.

"With hand work or with the usual fashion designing, I have something in my head that's three-dimensional, which first has to be translated into something two-dimensional, like a drawing, then it goes to three dimensionality again," van Herpen told the architecture and design magazine *Dezeen*. "It's a strange way of working—you have a step in between."

Van Herpen won the 2014 Andam Prize, one of the oldest and most lucrative fashion awards for young designers. The prize included €250,000 and a year of mentorship, among other perks.

Physics and motion, including the collisions at the Large Hadron Collider, have inspired van Herpen's dsigns.

established in 1815, released a collection of pieces in 2014 that incorporate panels of 3D-printed fabrics into otherwise traditionally produced knitwear.

There is a lot of progress to make in the realm of the materials and textures available for 3D-printed fabrics, but many anticipate that 3D-printed clothing will change the future of fashion and shopping.

"I think it's super old-fashioned that it's only the 100 richest women in the world who have clothes that actually fit them and I think 3D printing can really fill up a gap there," van Herpen said in an interview with the architecture and design magazine *Dezeen*. In a future with 3D-printed clothing widely available, van Herpen says, "everybody could have their own body scanned and just order clothes that fit perfectly."

Computing Advancements Behind 3D Printing

When 3D printing first came on the scene, 3D printers could only print in one material at a time. That limited the artistic potential of the medium (and impacted other industries as well). In 2013, the Massachusetts Institute of Technology's Computer Science and Artificial Intelligence Lab (CSAIL) released software that made it possible to not just print in multiple materials but to print materials of varying density and flexibility.

MIT's software was not the first to allow printing multiple materials in one object, but it did make it significantly easier from a computing perspective to do so. Previously, designing an object with multiple materials and other specifications such as texture or color created an enormous amount of data to store and process. MIT's software uses a software architecture design that computes and streams data on demand to the printer to reduce the amount of data that needs to be stored at any one time.

TECHNOLOGY, MUSIC, and FORGED PAINTINGS

Computer science has also transformed the possibilities for making music, from empowering humans to make music in new ways to creating computer programs that write their own music.

Technology Assisting Humans

The musician Imogen Heap has developed software and hardware for gesture-controlled gloves, called Mi.Mu. Instead of interacting directly with her computer on stage, the gloves allow her to more elegantly interact with her computer from afar to control the pitch, filters, and sounds of her music during performances. The gloves don't just enhance her remote control of her technology; they take advantage of the natural relationship between music and movement, much like a conductor moves to direct an orchestra of musicians.

Technology Making Music On Its Own

Computer scientists, including a team at Sony's Computer Science Lab in Paris, have built algorithms that can "compose" music in the style of famous musicians, such as Bach or John Coltrane. The music produced by these computer programs may be useful in commercial applications, such as shopping malls and other places.

Another team from the University of Malaga in Spain has built a computer named Iamus that composes chamber music in its own style (rather than songs that sound like the music of a great composer), including a score titled *Hello World*. (When a programmer tests a new program, it's traditional to use "hello world!" as the test message.) The

London Symphony Orchestra has performed Iamus's work in an album titled *Iamus,* the first full album composed by a computer and performed by humans.

According to *Time* magazine's music tech correspondent Matt Peckham in a January 2013 review of the album:

> It's not as formless as you'd think, nor does it sound as if Iamus' designers are employing the "contemporary" label as a gimmicky way to excuse the compositional mercurialness of their computer algorithm.
>
> Take the opener, "Tránsitos," which piles dense, gorgeously dissonant layers of instrumentation, punctuated by low bell-like sounds, to create a beautifully unsettling and yet entirely musical idea you'd be forgiven for confusing with something written for a despairing or terrifying moment in a film.

The music the computers write at the moment depends on human programming. It is, on its own, perhaps not very interesting. However, if computers are programmed to create music unlike anything humans currently create, there may be much more interesting computer-composed music on the horizon.

Computer Paintings That Imitate the Greats

Similar to computer-composed music, there is also computer-generated visual art, including a project begun in 2014 to release a new Rembrandt painting that was not created by Rembrandt himself, but by a computer in the style of Rembrandt. Computer scientists, art historians, and data analysts worked together to build a software program that could analyze common elements of Rembrandt's work and create a 3D-printed portrait similar to his previous work, down to the texture of his brushstrokes. The resulting portrait is good enough to prompt questions about the future applications of computer software to create art forgeries.

DRONE ART

The use of drones, or unmanned aircraft, has grown immensely in the last several years. Unmanned aircraft were used throughout the twentieth century largely for military purposes, such as guided German bombs in World War II. In 2010, Parrot introduced the first smartphone-controlled drone at the Consumer Electronics Show in Las Vegas. Today, drones are used for purposes ranging from storm tracking to monitoring and deterring poachers to agricultural pesticide application. In the art world, drones are opening up new avenues for photography and videography.

Drones are more than just remote-controlled devices. They contain tiny computers with sensors that give them information about their altitude, help them correct for gusts of wind, and sense the ground as they slowly land. Drones are programmed to be able to self-stabilize and hold GPS positions without a human controlling each motion.

Paired with a camera, drones allow videographers to capture footage in areas and angles otherwise inaccessible due to terrain, safety, or other limitations. Cinematographers have used drones to film movies including the James Bond film *Spectre* and *The Expendables 3*. Music videos from bands including OK Go rely on drone footage. With the falling cost of drones, smaller, independent videographers are entering the field as well. For example, photographer Nansen

The retail giant Amazon is developing a drone delivery service that could deliver packages in thirty minutes or less.

Weber was the first to use a drone to film the Northwest Passage, a sea route connecting the northern Atlantic and Pacific Oceans through the Arctic Ocean. The video footage skims low along the coastline and above the sea, showing a beluga whale nursery, a swimming polar bear, broken chunks of sea ice, and more of the environmentally significant but vulnerable region.

TEACHING COMPUTERS and ART

Many educational institutions, from art schools to computer science powerhouses, are combining education in computing and the arts. The California Institute of the Arts (CalArts) was founded in the 1960s by Walt Disney as an arts school where creative disciplines could inspire one another. Today, the school has a two-year master of fine arts program in art and technology. The program teaches art students how to use computer programming, networked systems, digital image and sound design, and more to bring technology into their art practice.

Stanford, meanwhile, introduced a joint major they call CS+X. The program, launched in 2014, offers degrees in computer science paired with art, comparative literature, music, foreign languages, and other humanities courses. Carnegie Mellon offers a "BXA" that combines computer science and fine arts for students interested in combining technology and the arts for fields such as game design, computer animation, robotic art, and more. Dartmouth, Yale, and numerous other universities offer similar programs.

From MACHINE WEAVING to PRINTING 3D ART

Throughout history, humans have sought to improve the creative process through new technology. That desire has propelled our culture from the Jacquard loom, the first instance of humans communicating instructions to machines, to computers that initially used the same punch card data input method as the Jacquard loom, to the sophisticated computers of today that we can use to design and print wearable garments and jewelry.

The new educational programs created by CalArts, Stanford, and others help ensure that artists are also technologists—and that computer scientists are also artists—so that art and technology can continue pushing each other forward for years to come.

GLOSSARY

abacus (plural **abaci**) A tool used for counting. The ancient abacus was a counting board with pebbles or other counters; a bead frame abacus developed centuries later and is still used in many Asian countries.

augmented reality Technology that layers computer-generated images over real-world views to create an altered view of reality.

binary A number system that represents all numeric values using the digits 1 and 0. Computers use binary code to store information.

bitmap A bitmap is a file that indicates the color, pixel by pixel, of regions on a display screen.

bulla (plural **bullae**) A clay pouch used by the ancient Sumerians that contained clay beads that represented amounts exchanged between people, eventually with amounts marked on the outside of the pouch.

calculi Counters used to represent amounts on ancient Roman counter board abaci. Calculi often came in a variety of materials, including bone, ivory, and glass.

cel Transparent sheets of celluloid (plastic) on which characters, objects, and scenes are drawn for traditionally animated films.

circuit In computing, the components that provide paths for electrical currents in computers. Integrated circuits include diodes, which control the flow of the current; transistors, which can be used as switches; and microprocessors, which tell the other components how to interact.

conditional branching A programming operation that tells the computer to move to another part of the program depending on the value present, often with "if-then" logic.

electromechanical A device with moving parts that is electrically operated, such as an electric typewriter and the very earliest computers.

graphical user interface A visual method of interaction between users and electronic devices that includes icons and other graphical indicators, such as a wastebasket for trashing documents.

Hindu-Arabic numerals The numbers 0 through 9, a system that originated in India and arrived in Europe via Middle Eastern scholars and texts.

loop In programming, a sequence of instructions that is repeated until a certain condition is met.

microprocessor A complete computation engine (like the brain of a computer) contained in a single chip, typically using a single integrated circuit. Since Intel sold the first microprocessor in 1971, microprocessors have gotten increasingly small, powerful, and affordable.

parchment A flat material made from the processed skin of an animal, often sheep. Parchment was used for writing on until it was replaced by paper in the late Middle Ages.

pictograph A pictorial representation of a word, number, or phrase; the earliest form of written numbers and words.

pixel From the term "picture element," the basic unit of programmable color on a display screen or computer image.

polymer A type of large molecule made of multiple repeating units. Examples include natural polymers, such as silk and wool, and synthetic polymers, such as synthetic rubber and silicone.

punch cards Cards with perforations (often rectangular holes) that are inserted into computers to communicate instructions. Punch cards were used to program and enter data into computers for much of the twentieth century.

relay switch An electromechanically operated switch found in early computers that uses a magnet to open and close a circuit. An advantage of using a relay switch is that it takes a small amount of power to operate a relay but the relay can control much more powerful devices.

shuttle In weaving, a tool that holds thread and, controlled by the weaver, carries that thread across the loom between other threads held fastened to the loom to weave cloth.

tally stick An ancient tool used to record numbers or amounts, initially made of animal bones and later made from wood.

transistor An electronic component that amplifies or switches electronic signals and electrical power; the foundation of modern electronics.

virtual reality A three-dimensional, computer-generated environment that users can interact with in a seemingly real way using equipment such as a headset.

warp In weaving, the set of threads fastened to the loom that can be lifted to alter the pattern.

weft In weaving, the thread held in the shuttle and drawn through the warp threads each time the weaver passes the shuttle across the loom, in doing so creating woven cloth from the threads.

BIBLIOGRAPHY

"The Art of 3D Printing." Smithsonian Channel. Retrieved May 25, 2016. http://www.smithsonianchannel.com/videos/the-art-of-3d-printing/20040.

Barrett, Claire. "Everybody Could Have Their Body Scanned and Order Clothes That Fit Perfectly." *Dezeen*, April 24, 2013. http://www.dezeen.com/2013/04/24/iris-van-herpen-interview.

Bellos, Alex. "Abacus Adds Up to Number Joy in Japan." *The Guardian*. October 25, 2012. https://www.theguardian.com/science/alexs-adventures-in-numberland/2012/oct/25/abacus-number-joy-japan.

Colombo, Jorge. "Field Work." Retrieved May 25, 2016. http://www.jorgecolombo.com/nyfpjc/index.htm.

Elmer-DeWitt, Philip. "Apple from 1980 to 2012." *Fortune*, October 5, 2012. http://fortune.com/2012/10/05/apple-from-1980-to-2012/.

Essinger, James. *Jacquard's Web.* Oxford, UK: Oxford University Press, 2004.

Fernandes, Luis. "The Abacus: A Brief History." January 11, 2015. http://www.ee.ryerson.ca/~elf/abacus/history.html.

Gottschalk, Molly. "Virtual Reality Is the Most Powerful Medium of Our Time." *Artsy*, March 16, 2016. https://www.artsy.net/article/artsy-editorial-virtual-reality-is-the-most-powerful-artistic-medium-of-our-time.

Isaacson, Walter. *The Innovators.* New York: Simon & Schuster, 2014.

———. *Steve Jobs.* New York: Simon & Schuster, 2011.

Jobs, Steve. "Steve Jobs' 2005 Stanford Commencement Address." June 12, 2005. https://www.youtube.com/watch?v=UF8uR6Z6KLc.

Knowlton, Kenneth. "A Computer Technique for the Production of Animated Movies." Retrieved May 25, 2016. https://www.youtube.com/watch?v=_Lmi6cmrq0w.

Levy, Steven. "The Macintosh Is 30, and I Was There for Its Birth." *Wired.* January 24, 2014. http://www.wired.com/2014/01/macintosh-30th-anniversary.

Lycett, Andrew. "Breaking Germany's Enigma Code." BBC. February 17, 2012. http://www.bbc.co.uk/history/worldwars/wwtwo/enigma_01.shtml.

Maslin, Janet. "Review/Film; Disney's 'Beauty and the Beast' Updated in Form and Content.'" *New York Times*, November 13, 1991.

"Numbers and Calculations with the Ancient Sumerians." *The Garden of Archimedes*. Retrieved May 25, 2016. http://php.math.unifi.it/archimede/archimede/laboratori/materiali/sumeriENG-giusti.pdf.

O'Brien, Jeffrey M. "The Race to Make Virtual Reality an Actual (Business) Reality." *Fortune*, May 1, 2016.

Peckham, Matt. "Finally, a Computer That Writes Contemporary Music Without Human Help." *Time*, January 4, 2013. http://techland.time.com/2013/01/04/finally-a-computer-that-writes-contemporary-music-without-human-help.

Pham, Alex. "Seven Ways iTunes Changed the Music Industry." *Billboard*, April 25, 2013. http://www.billboard.com/biz/articles/news/1559622/seven-ways-itunes-changed-the-music-industry.

Pullan, J. M. *The History of the Abacus*. New York: Frederick A. Praeger, 1969.

Raab, Josh. "Virtual Reality is for Artists." *Time*. Retrieved May 25, 2016. http://time.com/vr-is-for-artists.

"The Story of One." BBC, September 12, 2015. https://www.youtube.com/watch?v=0912nR3knYk.

Sutton, Gloria. *The Experience Machine: Stan VanDerBeek's Movie-Drome and Expanded Cinema.* Cambridge, MA: MIT Press, 2015.

"When a Bit Became a Pixel." Computer History Museum. Retrieved May 25, 2016. http://www.computerhistory.org/revolution/computer-graphics-music-and-art/15/intro/2398.

FURTHER INFORMATION

Books

Braddock Clarke, Sarah E. and Jane Harris. *Digital Visions for Fashion and Textiles: Made in Code*. New York: Thames & Hudson, 2012.

Ceruzzi, Paul E. *Computing: A Concise History*. Cambridge: MIT Press, 2010.

Frauenfelder, Mark. *The Computer: An Illustrated History from Its Origins to the Present Day*. London: Carlton Books, 2013.

Isaacson, Walter. *The Innovators: How a Group of Hackers, Geniuses, and Geeks Created the Digital Revolution*. New York: Simon & Schuster, 2014.

Paul, Christiane. *Digital Art*. 3rd ed. New York: Thames & Hudson, 2015.

Websites

The Computer History Museum

http://www.computerhistory.org/timeline/computers

This website includes a timeline of computer history that is organized by categories, including "Memory & Storage," "Software & Languages," and "Networking & the Web."

People Behind the Pizels: The History of Computer Graphics
http://www.historyofcg.com
Read biographies of major figures in the history of computer graphics. This site also includes descriptions of organizations and companies that have shaped the field.

VR Is for Artists
http://www.time.com/vr-is-for-artists
Watch seven established artists create art in virtual reality for the first time, and hear their reactions to what they've made.

Videos

A Primer on 3D Printing
http://www.ted.com/talks/lisa_harouni_a_primer_on_3d_printing?language=en#
Watch a TED talk on 3D printing and how the way we make things is changing.

Steve Jobs Talks About Toy Story Animation
http://www.youtube.com/watch?v=NvtebuKfZ5I
Hear about the history of movies from 1895 to 1995 as told by Steve Jobs as he introduces the first completely computer-generated animated film, *Toy Story*.

Punch Card Programming
http://www.youtube.com/watch?v=KG2M4ttzBnY
Learn about how programmers used punch cards from Professor David Brailsford, a professor of computer science at the University of Nottingham in the United Kingdom.

INDEX

Page numbers in **boldface** are illustrations. Entries in **boldface** are glossary terms.

ABOUT the AUTHOR

Rachel Keranen is a writer based in Madison, Wisconsin. Her work focuses on science, software, and entrepreneurship. She's passionate about learning and loves taking deep dives into science and history. In addition to the books that she writes, Keranen's previous work includes articles in the *Minneapolis/St. Paul Business Journal* and the *London Business Matters* magazine, as well as copywriting for tech companies. Keranen enjoys traveling, biking, and spending time near water.